GALOOTS WITH GUNS

Slowly, he got his feet underneath him and turned to look around and beyond the boulder.

Two shots broke the momentary calm, sending twin slugs toward Clint. One of the bullets blew high, while the other took a small piece out of Clint's cover, causing a chest-high shower of stone chips and sparks.

"Jesus," Clint muttered.

"Stick yer head out again, boy," yelled one of the shooters.

The other one's voice rang out, deeper and slower than his partner's. "Yeah . . . stick yer head out for us."

Clint could hear the stupidity in their voices.

Even better, Clint thought as he hefted the familiar weight of the modified Colt in his hand. *This shouldn't take long at all.*

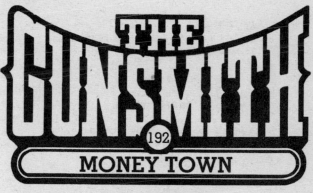

THE GUNSMITH

192

MONEY TOWN

J. R. ROBERTS

J

JOVE BOOKS, NEW YORK

MONEY TOWN

A Jove Book / published by arrangement with
the author

PRINTING HISTORY
Jove edition / December 1997

The Putnam Berkley World Wide Web site address is
http://www.berkley.com

ISBN: 0-515-12192-4

A JOVE BOOK®
Jove Books are published by The Berkley Publishing Group,
a member of Penguin Putnam Inc., 200 Madison Avenue,
New York, New York 10016.
JOVE and the "J" design are trademarks
belonging to Jove Publications, Inc.

PRINTED IN THE UNITED STATES OF AMERICA

10 9 8 7 6 5 4 3 2 1

THE GUNSMITH

192

MONEY TOWN

ONE

Taking a deep, slow breath Clint pulled in a lungful of fresh air. He'd been riding all day, stopping only after making his way across another of many barren stretches of trail across Wyoming. He was grateful for the short respite.

Clint looked over to check and see if his big black gelding, Duke, who was standing in the midst of an outcropping of trees, was all right.

He arched his back against the rough surface of the boulder he'd been leaning against as a cool breeze whipped around the rock and across his face. Slowly, he got his feet underneath him and turned to look around and beyond the boulder.

Two shots broke the momentary calm, sending twin slugs toward Clint. One of the bullets blew high, while the other took a small piece out of Clint's cover, causing a chest-high shower of stone chips and sparks.

"Jesus," Clint muttered as he jerked his body back into sitting position behind the large rock.

They were close, the sons of bitches. From his split-second peek, he'd spotted the two men standing behind a pair of sickly pines. Clint thought the men would have been smart enough to seek better cover and flank him, but his attackers seemed perfectly happy where they were.

They outnumbered him two-to-one and they thought that would be enough. Good, he thought, feeling better knowing he was up against a pair of cocky small-timers.

"Stick yer head out again, boy," yelled one of the shooters. "I ain't against comin' after ya, but I wouldn't mind you savin' me the trouble."

The other one's voice rang out, deeper and slower than his partner's. "Yeah . . . stick yer head out for us."

Clint could hear the stupidity in their voices. The gunmen sounded like nothing more than a couple of farm boys with Pa's rifle.

Even better, Clint thought as he hefted the familiar weight of the modified Colt in his hand. This shouldn't take long at all.

Again, Clint gathered himself into a crouched position and took a deep breath. On the exhale, he partially stood up, giving his attackers their wish by poking his head up into clear view.

Yelling excitedly the two snipers sent another volley of bullets toward their target. Just as the shooting started, however, Clint withdrew his head only to quickly poke it out from the other side of the boulder. In the same fluid motion, Clint swung his gun hand around and returned fire.

Still shooting at the same spot where Clint's head had first appeared, the two gunmen gave Clint a few precious seconds in which to pick his targets. The sound of Clint's Colt mixed with the rifle blasts as splinters exploded inches away from both of the snipers' faces.

"C'mon, Jed," the first sniper yelled, "he's right there."

Jed simply grunted. While he wasn't as excited as his partner by Clint's return of fire, neither was he afraid.

"Shut up, Clem," he shouted, "I know what I'm doin'."

Clint could tell the two men were shifting their aim to his new position. It was time to move unless he wanted to stay behind that boulder forever. Tucking into a tight ball, he rolled away from the rock and to his feet.

As though he were watching the fight as a spectator, Clint took in the scene with experienced eyes. Clem was the faster of the two and about to pull the trigger. That meant he got it first.

Aiming as though he were simply pointing his finger at the other man, Clint squeezed off a shot that tore through Clem's shoulder and spun him around like a toy. Suddenly, Clem didn't seem so excited anymore.

Clint's next shot hit Jed in the arm. It didn't put him down, but it was enough to prevent him from firing his weapon. The burning pain in his right arm caused Jed to swivel out of his firing position, putting the dead pine tree between himself and Clint.

Clint had one more bullet left before he had to reload. It looked like Jed was set on hiding for a little while, so Clint considered reloading before the action started again. Instead, he decided to do the job right.

Lowering his arm slightly, Clint sent his last round through the edge of Jed's brittle wooden cover and into the meaty part of the man's thigh. Jed dropped his rifle to grab his fresh wound before falling to the ground.

On the way over to pick up the discarded weapons of the two wounded gunmen, Clint caught the rustle of movement out of the corner of his eye. Before he could turn to look closer, a bullet zipped past his head, followed closely by the crack of a distant rifle.

"Damn!" Clint grunted as he leapt behind one of the dead pines. He'd been sure there were only— there were only supposed to be two! While reloading his gun Clint tried to figure out how he was going to keep an eye on the two men he'd put down as well as take care of the third.

"You need some help, here?"

Clint snapped his pistol closed, looked up, and aimed at whoever had snuck up on him. The shining silver star on the stranger's chest saved his life.

"It's about time you showed up," Clint said, speaking more to the star than to the man. "Bill told me you were supposed to meet me an hour ago."

"Sorry about that."

"What about the other one? I think he's up on that ridge," Clint said, motioning in the direction of the gunshot. "There wasn't supposed to be three."

The sheriff, casually leading his horse over to where Jed and Clem were lying, didn't even turn to look where Clint was pointing.

"That's one of my boys. He's got an itchy trigger finger. He probably just didn't recognize you."

"We got them, Sheriff," said a voice from nearby.

"Good work. Bring them on in." After tying the hands of the two gunmen, the sheriff turned his attention back to Clint.

"I know who these two are, but I've never seen you before."

Clint holstered his gun and walked over to where Duke was standing. He took the gelding's reins and walked back over to where the sheriff was standing.

"I'm a friend of Bill Henderschott's. My name is—"

"Save it," the sheriff said, cutting him off. "Come

into town with me and tell it to me there."

Just then the two sheriff's deputies appeared next to the sheriff. They had tossed the two bound and wounded gunmen over their horses like two sacks of flour. Both men still had their guns drawn and held them loosely pointed in Clint's direction.

None of the lawmen seemed at all pleased that Clint had done their jobs for them. More than that, they seemed to be waiting for an excuse to tie him up and throw him up on his horse, alongside Jed and Clem.

"Put your guns up and let's go," the sheriff said to his men. He looked at Clint. "These two need a doctor, and I guess you'll be wanting the reward money for bringing them in."

"I don't want any mon—" Clint started, but the lawman cut him off again.

"I said save it, mister," the sheriff said angrily. "You can have your say when we get to my office."

"Yeah," Clint said to himself. "We've got some things to discuss."

TWO

The town of Cedar Cross, Wyoming, had nothing to live up to either of the images that came to mind when Clint heard the name. Built in the middle of a barren grassland, there were no trees anywhere near the town limits. Also, with only one street and no proper church, there was nothing crossing anything.

The two captured shooters seemed content sitting tied up over the backs of their horses and only spoke angrily to each other during the ride. Each seemed to be blaming the other for their misfortunes. Clint wasn't familiar with the pair, but he knew enough about them to realize that they wouldn't be hatching any brilliant plans for escape anytime soon.

He kept Duke alongside the sheriff's horse all the way back to town. The ride, only about five miles, seemed longer due to the silence the sheriff seemed to want to keep.

The only sound as they rode into town was a

chuckle from Clint as he saw that the city planners had taken the trouble to label Cedar Cross's only street with a large, ornate sign. Apparently, if you could only have one street, it had to be Main Street.

The sheriff still didn't take his eyes off the road ahead and brought the party to a stop at a small shack at the town's halfway point, on the left side of Main Street. The tall, muscular sheriff dismounted and signaled for his younger deputies to take their prisoners inside.

The shack, looking as though it would fall down in the first stiff breeze, would have looked like any other poorly erected house were it not for the sign over the door that read: JAMES PARKER, SHERIFF. Neither of the deputies could have been more than twenty years old, but they dragged Jed and Clem off their mounts and into the sheriff's office with quiet professionalism.

Watching with dark, squinting eyes while his men worked, the sheriff stood quietly, ignoring Clint completely.

"I think you owe me some sort of explanation, Parker," Clint said.

The lawman's head snapped around. "You'll call me Sheriff, mister!"

Instead of shaking in his boots, Clint stood toe-to-toe with the lawman and let his anger surface.

"I'll call you sheriff when you start acting like one! You were supposed to meet me at that spot long before those two showed up. Instead, you nearly got me killed."

A crowd was starting to form, gathering a safe distance away from the sheriff and the stranger who dared to fight with him. Looking around, Parker noticed the gaping townfolk and grabbed Clint by the elbow.

"Let's take this inside."

Clint pulled away from the sheriff's grip without

breaking the hard stare leveled at the man. Without a word, he followed Parker into the small wooden building, and one of the deputies slammed the door shut behind him.

Inside, Parker turned on him quickly.

"I've had men thrown in jail for less than that more than once!" he snapped.

"Then that means you've abused the power of your office more than once."

"Bill Henderschott told me you were a good man, so I'll let that outburst go for now, but don't you ever talk to me like that again—especially in public. I have to have the respect of these people."

Clint was fuming and it took all his resolve to keep from hauling off and knocking the sheriff to the floor. After a few moments of silence he had collected himself enough to talk to the man again.

"Bill told me the same thing about you, Parker. He said you were a good lawman, and that you'd be a man I could count on to watch my back." Clint paced the room, and both of the young deputies shuffled out of his way. They had been watching the heated exchange between the two men with fascination. They still did not know exactly who Clint was.

"All you had to do was show up on time and we could have taken them without firing a shot," Clint said. "Next thing I know, I'm the one being shot at."

Sheriff Parker stood with his arms folded across his chest, staring straight at Clint. "They got away from us. Besides," he said, "you were miles away from where we were supposed to meet. I was lucky I found you at all, the way those two got the drop on you."

"They weren't even supposed to be there! I know we've never met before, Sheriff," Clint said, "but those idiots couldn't get the drop on a corpse. Hell, these two deputies of yours could have done a better job."

"Where do you know Bill from, anyway?"

"I've met Marshal Henderschott on several occasions, and I happened to be around when he was forming a posse to catch those two."

The sheriff strode across the room to his cluttered desk and sat down. After lighting up a thin cigar and propping his feet on top of the papers and other junk covering the desktop, Parker seemed more than confident. He was a man in his own element.

"Oh yeah, that's right," Parker said. "The Gunsmith to the rescue. Well, I've heard all kinds of stories about you, Adams, and you haven't lived up to my expectations either."

The two deputies gaped openly at Clint, now that they knew who he was.

"On second thought, I've never seen you before. How do I know you're really Clint Adams?"

Clint walked over to the desk and leaned over the piles of scattered papers and the man's feet to look Parker square in the eyes.

"You've got a star on your shirt, but that doesn't necessarily make you the Sheriff James Parker I was supposed to meet."

Sheriff Parker stared back at Clint, sizing him up while the deputies looked on nervously. They were still staring at Clint, as were the two men in the cells. They seemed stunned that they had been firing their guns at a legend, and had survived.

Swinging his feet to the floor, Parker came around his desk to stand next to Clint. He seemed calm now, in complete control of himself.

"Look, Adams," he said reasonably, "this whole thing got out of hand and we both lost our tempers. There's no need for us to squabble like this when the job got done anyway, right?"

Clint nodded and backed off a step.

The sheriff started walking toward the door.

"What matters now is that these two are behind

bars. Why don't you get yourself a drink and something to eat, and a hotel room, and I'll be by later
with your reward money."

"Keep the money, Parker," Clint said. "Just let me
know when Marshal Henderschott gets to town."

"He should be here tomorrow, or the next day, to
pick up these two. Meanwhile, I'll have a doctor look
at them. They should be happy they lived through an
encounter with you, huh?" The sheriff opened the
door to his office.

"Whatever," Clint said. "Just make sure these two
geniuses don't give you the slip again."

With that Clint walked through the open door and
collected Duke from in front of the office. Leading
the black gelding down the street to the livery stable,
he hoped his visit to Cedar Cross would be a short
one.

Clint was annoyed with Sheriff Parker more than
angry. Sure, the man had let two morons get away
from him, but Clint had allowed them to get the drop
on him. For that he felt foolish and annoyed with
himself. That hurt Clint's pride more than anything
else. Thinking about it after he handed Duke over to
the liveryman, Clint was still fuming as he walked
toward Cedar Cross's one hotel.

THREE

A town not used to having visitors, Cedar Cross had only one hotel and the owners hadn't even bothered to name it. The two-level building was three down from the sheriff's office and on the opposite side of the street. From the rickety porch just outside the hotel's lobby Clint could see the spread of the entire town. It wasn't much of a sight.

With his gear slung over his shoulder, Clint entered the dusty lobby and cleared his throat to wake up the desk clerk. The short, withered old man looked up from his nap and regarded Clint with clouded eyes.

"I need a room for the night," Clint said, breaking the silence.

The old-timer got painfully to his feet.

"Two dollars a night."

Clint swept a trail through the dust on the desktop

with his finger. Looking distastefully up the beat-up
stairs, he started to shake his head.

"A bit high, don't you think?"

"Includes breakfast every mornin'," the old man
said, as if that made all the difference in the world.

Clint was already tired of wasting time in this town
and decided not to try to bargain with the old man.
Not looking forward to the state the rooms must be
in, he'd be damned if he'd eat in the filthy place, as
well. He threw the money down on the desk for the
first night and looked for a register. Instead, all he
got was a rusty key.

"First door on yer left. Breakfast's at eight. If you
miss it, you gotta get it someplace else."

That was like having a whorehouse madam tell
you if you missed getting the clap in her house you'd
have to get it someplace else.

The room was every bit as grimy as Clint had pic-
tured it, and he decided to spend as much time away
from it as he could. After storing his gear and taking
a quick rest, he headed back downstairs and out onto
Main Street. The old man was asleep again.

After Clint left the sheriff's office, the two deputies
sprang to life. One of them, nineteen and wearing a
double rig, ran to the window to watch Clint lead his
horse to the livery.

He turned and looked at Parker.

"Was that really the Gunsmith, Sheriff?"

Sheriff Parker was back behind his desk with his
feet up again.

"Yeah, that's him, all right."

The other deputy, older than the first by two years,
planted himself on a stool in front of the jail cell.

"You could have told us we'd be meeting him. You
just told us he was Marshal Henderschott's friend."

"He *is* Bill's friend," Parker said. "Besides, I didn't

want you two getting all worked up when you heard who we were meeting. Turned out the man ain't all he's cracked up to be, anyway."

The deputy by the window turned to face the sheriff and took his hands off his pistols for the first time since Clint had raised his voice to the sheriff.

"What happened out there, Sheriff? How come he didn't meet us like he was supposed to?"

Staring off into space, Parker shook his head and mulled over the young man's question. He dropped his feet from the desk, grabbed a telegram from his desk.

"I don't know, Kyle. That's what's bothering me. Adams is supposed to be a good man . . . an ex-lawman . . . and I've heard nothing to make me think otherwise."

Holding up the telegram, Parker sat forward and reread the document.

"More than likely Marshal Henderschott will be coming by tomorrow to pick up his prisoners. This whole thing was his plan. He's the one who has to explain why it went wrong."

Then Parker stood up, threw the telegram onto the pile of papers on his desk, and glanced at Jed and Clem Barrows behind bars.

"It doesn't really matter whose fault it was, though, as long as we got our men. These things happen, boys," he said to the young deputies. "Even to the best of us."

FOUR

Walking through the entire town took Clint all of fifteen minutes. There were three restaurants, a saloon, and one general store. Clint picked one of the restaurants and went inside.

The place felt like the inside of someone's home and the food actually smelled pretty good. Taking a seat along the wall, Clint made sure he was away from the window, not so much because he feared for his safety, but so he wouldn't have to look outside. After a short wait, the waitress came over to Clint and set a cup of coffee in front of him.

"Welcome to Red's," she said. "What can I get for ya?"

She was short, had light red hair, and was a little overweight, but not so much as to make her unattractive. Underneath the simple brown dress and white apron, she looked full, plump, and soft. Be-

14

tween her and the appetizing smells in the air, Clint's mood started to brighten.

"Are you Red?" he asked.

She smiled a little, but not much. She must have heard the question a hundred times.

"No, Red's the cook. What are you hungry for?"

"How about a well-done steak and some potatoes? Oh, and do you have any biscuits?"

"Fresh this mornin'."

"I'll have some of those, then." Clint flashed the redhead a smile and looked around. He was the only customer in the place. "It seems like a slow time of day. Why don't you join me?"

For the first time the waitress turned her head to look at him straight on. Her face was pale, with a light range of freckles across her cheeks. As she turned, her long hair fell in wisps over her shoulders, making her look even better than she'd first appeared.

"Maybe," she said with a little grin, and left it at that.

Waiting for the food to arrive, Clint enjoyed the dead quiet of Red's. With a town this small he was surprised there was more than one restaurant. If this was any indication of the crowds that came through, Red either had to be independently wealthy or a lot busier on other days to make any kind of a living.

Clint took his first sip of coffee and decided on the notion that Red had some other business going. With the rancid taste still swirling in his mouth, Clint saw the little redhead coming out of the kitchen with a plate in her hands, still steaming from the stovetop.

"Here's our steak and biscuits," she said, setting the meal in front of Clint. "We're all out of potatoes. Can I get anything else for ya?"

Clint looked her up and down. Underneath the dress there was obviously a full, rounded body. Soft,

fleshy hips curved up to a thinner waist, which
sloped out again into a pair of ample breasts, the tops
of which were visible thanks to the low cut of her
dress and covered with a fine, shiny layer of sweat.

Staring down at him with blue eyes, she placed her
hands on her hips and waited for Clint's reply.

"Sure," Clint said. "You can pull up a chair and
join me."

The waitress took one step closer and leaned
down close to his ear, giving him a generous view of
her plump breasts. Looking into his eyes, she regarded Clint as though he were sitting on top of a
dung heap.

"I think you can do just fine on your own, mister."
Her tone was just right to make the hairs on the back
of Clint's neck stand up. Then, after a quick turn, she
headed back into the kitchen.

Right when the anger had been starting to fade,
and his mood had begun to lift, it had come crashing
back down on him, thanks to a terrible cup of coffee
and a testy waitress.

Normally, he didn't let rejection by a woman get
to him. After all, there were so many of them, and
most of them said yes. But that comment was the
last thing he had wanted or expected to hear.

And on top of that, his steak was cooked wrong.

FIVE

While on his nightly rounds Sheriff Parker happened to catch a glimpse of Clint standing at the bar in the saloon. Probably the best built establishment in town, the High Card still looked as if it had been constructed in fifteen hurried minutes. Even Sheriff Parker sometimes thought the whole town looked ready to collapse.

Inside, the poker tables were empty and there were only three other people in the place besides Clint and the bartender. Knowing every man in town on sight as he did, Clint Adams was easy to spot, and Parker decided to go in and have a word with him.

The bartender, a friendly-looking, middle-aged man missing his left arm, walked to the end of the bar closest to the door and smiled at the lawman. All the drinkers were imbibing quietly, insuring a long and boring night. The bartender was happy to see someone he could talk to.

"Evening, Sheriff," the barkeep said. "The usual?"

"Sounds good, Lee."

At the mention of the sheriff's presence, Clint looked up from his mug of beer. Parker picked up his beer and took it to the end of the bar where Clint was standing.

"Can I help you, Sheriff?" Clint asked, without giving the man a chance to settle in next to him.

Parker laughed under his breath and took a sip of his beer.

"Oh, it's 'Sheriff' now, is it?"

Clint didn't rise to the bait.

"I just wanted to see how you found Cedar Cross," Parker said.

"It wasn't that hard to find," Clint said. "It's all within sight of the front door of the hotel."

"Yeah, it's small," Parker agreed, "but it's quiet, and it's got potential to grow."

"I'm afraid I won't be around long enough to see that happen."

With that said Clint went back to his beer. He took a sip, then seemed surprised when he looked up and saw the sheriff still there.

"I also thought I'd apologize for that little mix-up we had today."

Clint thought of it as a little bit more than just a "mix-up," but he waited to allow the sheriff to go on.

"You've been a lawman so you'll understand when I tell you I had no intention of letting those boys get the drop on you like that. Things just got . . . mixed up."

That seemed to be a phrase the lawman liked.

Clint cocked his head to one side to regard Parker out of the corner of his eye.

"It was your job to meet me and cover me. Instead, I wound up getting ambushed and had to handle the whole matter myself."

"You had little trouble with those men, Adams,"

Parker said. "Fact is, they couldn't have bested you on their finest day, and you know it."

"That's not the point." Clint was getting frustrated again, and he didn't like the feeling. He fought to keep his voice down and not cause another scene.

"Bill told me I'd be covered and I believed him. Call me crazy, but nearly getting my head shot off during a posse run that should have been a cakewalk tends to get me upset."

Parker leaned back and watched Clint fume, and couldn't help but laugh. When he did, he got a look from Clint in return that would have stopped any man dead in his tracks.

"I'm sorry, Adams, but this is the most trouble those Barrows boys have ever caused in their lives and that's counting the two banks they tried to rob."

Clint looked back down at his drink, shook his head, and started to laugh as well.

"You're right. I probably wouldn't have minded as much if they'd just taken a shot at me in the street."

Turning to face Parker, Clint raised his glass in a magnanimous gesture.

"Here's to mix-ups, then."

"They happen to the best of us," the sheriff said, echoing the words he'd spoken to his deputies earlier in the day.

After the two drank to the statement Clint saw Sheriff Parker in a new light. The man hadn't acted any differently than any lawman would have in the same situation. Besides, he had no reason to believe he'd been purposely set up. Sitting there next to the man, Clint remembered all the good words Marshal Henderschott had had for Parker. Bill had always been a good judge of men.

"I guess the problem with having a reputation like mine," Clint said over a second round of drinks, "is that you start to believe it yourself. Having fools like the Barrows brothers get that close to killing me just doesn't sit right."

Parker shook his head and then bent it to sip some beer.

"They didn't get that close, Adams," he said. "I managed to see a bit of your shooting, and I'd say maybe I could start to believe your reputation, myself."

He downed his second beer in a few long gulps and stood up.

"I've spent enough time here. Got to finish my rounds. I could meet you here in the morning with Bill, see that you get your posse fee, even if you don't want the reward."

Clint looked at the bartender.

"You serve breakfast here?"

The bartender shrugged and said, "I can still flip a flapjack or two with my good arm. Can't promise it's the best in town, though. That'd be Red's."

"The service is friendlier here," Clint said. "I'll take my chances on the food."

SIX

Clint's bed turned out to be one step above sleeping on the ground. If he hadn't waited until he was dead tired to try to get some sleep, he wouldn't have been able to make it through the night. As it was, when the sun came up next morning, he felt as though he'd spent the night draped over a rock.

Feeling every painful move he made while getting dressed, he decided to save himself the walk to the High Card and have breakfast at the hotel. Besides, he thought, how bad could it be?

Ten minutes later he had the answer to that question and was on his way to the High Card. The smell of hot pancakes and coffee drifted in the air. Every one of the six felt-covered poker tables and two faro tables were empty and covered.

Although he thought he could hear movement from the rooms upstairs, nobody showed their faces beyond the banister overlooking the bar. At the same

21

time the bartender, Lee, appeared from the kitchen, one of the upstairs doors opened and a tousled brunette peeked outside. Seeing that it was only one man for breakfast she quickly ducked inside and went back to bed.

"Mornin'," Lee said. "They serve a complimentary breakfast at the hotel, you know."

Clint stretched his back and tried to rub some of the sleep from his eyes.

"Yeah, I caught a whiff of that free meal and I think I know why they're trying to give it away." Taking another healthy smell of the delicious aroma in the air, Clint smiled. "I think I made the right choice."

"I hope you feel that way after you taste it," Lee said, standing there with a large plate that was overflowing with huge, fluffy flapjacks and strips of bacon. After setting it down in front of Clint, he went back to the kitchen to fetch a jug of syrup and a cup of coffee.

"Enjoy," he said, when it was all on the table.

His mouth too filled to reply, Clint nodded as he quickly devoured the breakfast. After his plate was cleared, he sat back to savor another cup of coffee. It was the best he had felt since he had set out on the trail three days ago.

While Clint had been eating, Lee was getting ready for business, uncovering all the gaming tables. By the time nine a.m. rolled around the High Card was ready for another day—but another day of what? Clint wondered. When he'd left last night, close to midnight, there still wasn't much going on in the way of business.

Lee took a seat at Clint's table, with a cup of coffee of his own.

"So, what brings you to Cedar Cross?"

"A posse."

Clint shook his head at the alarmed look on Lee's face.

"Don't worry. I was part of the posse, not one of the men they were after."

"Did you find yer man?"

"We did, both of them, although it didn't go quite the way I planned, but yeah, we got them."

The rest of the morning passed as Clint took a leisurely stroll around town—again and again—killing time until the arrival of Bill Henderschott. By the early afternoon Cedar Cross actually looked pretty busy. Several men were passing through on their way to or from various expeditions in the area, hunting or otherwise, and townspeople were going to or from their chores, giving Main Street a fairly busy look.

To keep himself occupied while he waited for Henderschott he went back to the High Card, sat down at one of the poker tables with a deck of cards, and waited for some interested parties to enter. He ended up playing solitaire for a couple of hours before two other men—and then a third—joined him for a low-stakes game.

Clint was dealing when Bill Henderschott finally walked in. He completed the hand—winning it—and then announced that he was out.

"You're ahead," a man said.

"Oh, yeah," Clint said, "ten dollars. That break anybody?"

None of the three men answered.

"Thanks for the game."

He went to the bar, got a beer, and then walked over to sit with Marshal Bill Henderschott.

SEVEN

Henderschott was forty-six years old and had the rugged build of a mountain man. Standing just over six feet, he wore his bulk mostly in layers of grizzled muscle, but also had a slight paunch brought about from city life. His face was beaten and covered with a scraggly beard that hid several scars and many pockmarks. When he spoke, the booming voice fit in perfectly with what one would expect.

"Adams, I hear you're getting soft in your old age! Those boys give you a run for your money?"

Although Clint had met and seen Henderschott several times before, the other man felt comfortable addressing him like a long lost comrade. While he couldn't help but like the big man, Clint was content to keep Henderschott a friendly but infrequent acquaintance.

"Hello, Bill."

Slapping Clint on the shoulder, Bill grabbed ahold

of his beer and ordered another. He handed the second mug to Clint and spoke in a voice that seemed to echo around the room.

"I told you those Barrows boys would be ready for a fight, didn't I? How'd they get in back of ya?"

"Have you talked with Sheriff Parker?"

"Stopped by there first thing. He said you held your own, but ol' Jed Barrows got off the first shot. That don't sound like the Gunsmith I know from Wichita."

Clint was tired of thinking about the whole thing and just wanted to finish his business in Cedar Cross.

"Yeah, well," he said, "they got lucky, Bill. It happens."

"I hear ya," Henderschott said as he turned to take a look around the saloon. The saloon was the most crowded with people it had been since Clint's arrival. Among the people gathered around the gaming tables were cowhands and prospectors, mixed in among the locals. Mingling in with the crowd were a number of working girls, who finally deemed the business worth their while to emerge from the rooms upstairs. A busty blonde in a red dress seemed to catch Henderschott's eye, and she was quick to notice and respond with a wink and a smile.

The marshal downed the rest of his beer and pushed himself away from the bar. After taking a few steps toward the blonde, he stopped and turned to face Clint.

"I almost forgot," he said. "This is yours."

Henderschott pulled some folded bills out of his shirt pocket and slapped them on the bar in front of Clint. "There's your posse fee. Ya did a good job, Clint. I'm gonna be busy for the next few hours, maybe the night, so if I don't see ya before I leave town it was nice workin' with ya again."

Clint pocketed the money, even though he didn't

want it, and clapped Bill Henderschott on the shoulder.

"Likewise, Marshal. I'll check in with you next time I'm in Wichita."

Which wouldn't be for a long time, if he could help it. He'd done this simply as a favor to Henderschott, and it had gone bad.

Henderscott walked across the room to the blonde in the red dress. Clint swung back to the bar and took another sip of his beer before Henderschott came walking back to him, this time with the blonde on his arm.

"One more thing," he said. "I almost left without giving you a message from an old acquaintance of yours."

Not expecting word from anyone he knew, Clint said, "Oh, who?"

The marshal leaned in close, as if he was imparting some great secret.

"A lady told me that you and she were very good friends."

That didn't narrow things down for Clint any.

"Her name is Jeanette Colvin," Henderschott continued. "She's staying in Denver for the time being and told me to ask you to pay her a visit. Now seems to be as good a time as any, don't you think? Take care, Adams." The man tipped his hat and headed for the back stairway in the blonde's perfumed wake.

Clint laughed as he watched Henderschott chase after the busty blonde and follow her up to her room. Sometimes the man acted more like a cowboy than a lawman. Suddenly, with Jeanette Colvin in his thoughts, Clint was in a better mood.

The last time he'd seen her, she was trying to start her own dry goods store in Salt Lake City. They'd only known each other for a short time when Clint had passed through town over a year ago, but the brief encounter had been more than memorable for him. Apparently, she felt the same way.

With nothing on his agenda besides putting Cedar Cross behind him, Clint was eager to get on the trail to Denver. The clean mountain air had always agreed with him and that, combined with his fond memories of Jeanette, was all the excuse he needed to take some time for himself in the Rockies.

After finishing his beer Clint left some money for Lee and headed toward Sheriff Parker's office. He thought he should check in just to make sure everything was well in hand.

"No problems here," Parker said. "Marshal Henderschott already came by and will be taking them back to Wichita tomorrow morning. Will you be staying any longer?"

Clint was still standing in the doorway to the office, itching to leave.

"No. I'm fixing to leave in the morning. I'd leave now, but it's a little late to get started. I've got some . . . business to take care of in Denver. It was . . . uh, interesting, Sheriff."

"Will you be catching the stage to Denver, or riding?"

"I was thinking of riding, but when does the stage arrive?"

"It'll get in late today, and then leave again in the morning."

Clint thought about it. He'd ridden Duke pretty hard in his pursuit of the Barrows brothers.

"Maybe I will take the stage."

"The office is right down the street, if you want to get a ticket, but they're closed now. You'll have to do it early in the morning."

"I think I will, Sheriff," Clint said. "I think I will."

He could hitch Duke to the back of the stage. Making the trip with nobody on his back would be like giving the big gelding a rest.

"Have a good trip," Parker said. "Stop in if you're ever passing by."

No chance, Clint thought as he left the office. Not a chance in hell.

As he walked back to the hotel Clint swore he could smell Jeanette's sweet skin and feel her silky hair, even though it had been more than a year since he'd actually had that pleasure.

Seeing her, Clint decided, would be his true reward for all the hassle he'd been put through over the past few days. The message from Jeanette had taken him completely by surprise, making him all but forget the Barrows brothers and the posse fee folded up in his pocket.

EIGHT

On the second day of riding on the hard, jostling seat inside the stage, Clint was getting overly anxious to end the uncomfortable journey and arrive in Denver. According to the driver they should be at their destination before dusk. The terrain was becoming rocky and steep, with every bump in the road making its presence known to the rattled travelers.

Besides Clint the Denver stage was carrying a young couple on their way to their honeymoon and a small, weathered man who said no more than a few words during the trip.

To take her mind off of the unpleasant ride, the new bride busied herself trying to make small talk with her fellow passengers, talking the ear off of anyone who could hear her over the horses' pounding hooves.

"We just got married four days ago," the fragile-looking girl announced.

Clint forced a smile on his face, because the other man was ignoring her.

"So you've said."

The girl couldn't have been more than eighteen and had the wide-eyed look of a pretty, small-town belle. Her curly golden hair bounced with every jolt of the stage, yet her firm young body only moved slightly underneath the pink cotton dress. Clint had had plenty of time over the past couple of days to examine the girl sitting directly across from him. Even if she was married, she made a pleasant distraction.

"John's family has some land in the mountains and he just knows there's gold to be found. Isn't that right, dear?"

John was the husband and, by this point in the trip, he was beginning to sleep more. The last few times his wife had started talking he'd rolled his eyes and turned to look out the window.

"Sure, that's right, Ellie," he said.

For the first time during the trip the small man sitting next to Clint looked up from his usual downward stare. His face was dirty and a pair of scars made a crude "X" over his left cheek. The body underneath the dusty trail clothes was bulky, and muscular arms protruded from grimy, rolled up sleeves.

"Did you say gold?" he asked.

Ellie looked surprised, but not enough to make her speechless.

"Yes, sir," she said. "John's a miner. We met when he was cashing in the first nugget he ever found."

Turning to the man next to him, Clint tried to strike up a conversation, if only just to hear a different voice for a while. "What brings you to Denver?"

The grimy man shifted uncomfortably in his seat and said, "Business."

"What kind of business?"

The man gave him a slow look and said, "My business."

Clint took that as a dismissal and a signal that the man really didn't want to start talking, after all. He turned his attention back to Ellie's bright, smiling face. By this time, with the hard trail and even harder seats, even the drivers seemed to be losing their steam. She seemed to be the only one who was fresh. Clint had been on several stagecoaches but had never been on one that felt so close to falling apart before. He decided then and there that he'd stick to riding Duke, or a train, but there would be no more stages.

Ellie started in on a story that her momma used to tell her back home when Clint came to the conclusion that her husband had the right idea. Slowly, he leaned back and pulled his hat down over his eyes. As Clint drifted off to sleep, Ellie never stopped her story.

He wasn't sure how much time had passed before being roused from his slumber. For a change, John was up and alert and Ellie was asleep. Clint rubbed his eyes and looked out the window to see what John was staring intently at. Next to him the grimy man's face was also intent and focused on what was going on outside.

Alongside the stage rode a pair of men on brown horses. Their rifles were in plain sight and held casually, propped up on their thighs. The rider in the lead was keeping even with the driver, motioning for him to stop. Staying behind the coach, close enough to cover his partner, the second man watched carefully for any sign of trouble. He was in a position where he could easily pick off the driver, the man riding shotgun, or anyone in the coach.

Clint could tell these men knew what they were doing.

After a few shouted words between the lead rider

and the stage driver, the team was reined to a stop, with the backup rider staying in position to cover his partner. When the first horseman swung down off his mount, Clint had a hard time making out the details of the man's features. Besides standing with the sun at his back, the man's entire body was covered with a thick layer of trail dust.

"C'mon out, Gentry," the dismounted rider called. "You know why we're here, so let's get it over with."

The quiet man, now visibly nervous, grunted under his breath before throwing open the stagecoach door and climbing out.

"At least now we know his name," John whispered to his wife, who had woken up when the stage stopped.

Clint was busy trying to determine the intentions of the men who'd stopped the stage. Although they were both armed and keeping a safe distance from the coach, neither looked anxious to fight. Clint's hand reflexively went to his Colt, but he decided to wait for the mysterious men to make the first move.

Standing in the blazing sun, talking to the first rider, the man called Gentry didn't look as small as he had when he was slumped inside the coach, but he still stood a few inches shorter than the man who had called him out. As he spoke and gestured wildly, Gentry never looked away from the lead rider, who simply nodded and waited for him to finish.

John craned his neck to get a better look at the people outside but was hesitant to stick his head out the window.

"Do you think they know each other?" he asked.

"Seems that way," Clint said.

"Shouldn't we do something?"

"Like what?" Clint asked. "If they've got business of some kind, let them do it. As long as their affairs don't cause any harm, we should stay out of them."

Still, Clint's hand never strayed very far from his

gun, which he was ready to use at the first sign of trouble. However, the men outside did no more than talk for a minute or so before Gentry apparently ran out of wind.

Now, with his eyes adjusting to the direct sunlight, Clint could barely make out the other man's face. It was his turn to talk and he did so without moving anything but his lips. The only gesture he made was to motion toward his partner, who was now positioned by the front of the stage where he had everybody in sight.

Gentry seemed to contemplate his situation for a few seconds before shrugging and turning toward the stage. He got a foothold on one of the wheel rims and stretched to retrieve one of his bags from the top of the coach. Handing the bulky carpetbag down to the first rider, Gentry hopped off the wheel and waited.

Clint could now make out the black clothing both riders wore beneath their battered dusters. With the sun in just the wrong spot, however, he couldn't make out much more. The first rider took a few moments to examine the contents of Gentry's bag before nodding to his partner. After that, he slapped the smaller man on the back, hooked the bag onto his saddle horn, and lifted himself onto his horse.

Gentry climbed back into the stage and the team was once again urged forward, while both horsemen stayed put to watch the stage depart. After they were reduced to two specks in the distance, Clint saw the men turn their horses and take off in the opposite direction.

Next to Clint, Gentry stewed in his accustomed silence. Although he wanted to question the man about what the hell had happened back there, Clint decided to wait for a bit to let him cool off.

The sullen man was obviously mad as hell and they

still had a long day's drive ahead of them.

"What was that all about, I wonder?" the young wife asked, possessing none of Clint's reserve.

The smaller man did not even look at her.

NINE

The stage was five miles out of Denver before the man known as Gentry said another word.

"Is Gentry your first or last name?" Clint asked.

Sitting quietly, the sullen man next to Clint remained staring out the window with his arms folded across his chest. For the last two hours Clint had been trying to make conversation with the man without any success. Finally, Gentry's shell cracked.

"Last," he said.

Clint was shocked by the response—at the fact that there *was* a response—because he had been starting to think the man didn't have a voice.

"What's your first name?"

Turning, he looked at Clint with suspicion tinged with disgust.

"My name is Arlo Gentry, and I'd like a little quiet so I can try to get some sleep."

John chuckled to himself and received a scornful

look from his new wife. Since she'd awakened after the coach was stopped, her supply of stories had seemed to run dry and she had been alternately whispering to her husband and fanning herself.

"I don't see how anybody can sleep now," John said. "Either the road's gotten worse or this stage is falling apart."

Ellie shifted uncomfortably.

"I'd say the latter. This ride has been dreadful."

"Nevertheless," Gentry said, "I'm not one for discussions." With that he pulled his hat down over his eyes and tilted his chin to his chest. Sleep or not, the conversation was obviously over.

When they arrived in Denver, Clint was extremely grateful to be able to stretch his legs and feel his blood flowing again. The trip had served to remind him why he never traveled by stage.

Gentry jumped down to the ground and yanked one small bag from the luggage, which had been piled on the ground next to the stage, and promptly disappeared into one of the nearby buildings. Clint stood back and let the newlyweds retrieve their luggage before stepping to pick up his own things.

Approaching the driver, who was unloading a strongbox and two sacks of mail, Clint asked, "Are you staying on in Denver?"

The driver spoke without breaking his smooth, practiced motions. "Yep. For a day, anyway. Then we'll be movin' on to Leadville."

"You get stopped along the road much?"

Pausing to look at Clint this time, the driver seemed confused for a moment.

"Oh," he said finally, "you mean like earlier? Nah, those marshals just needed to talk to one of the passengers, is all."

"U.S. marshals?"

"That's what their badges said. The leader's a good man, but I never saw the deputy before."

From what he had seen of the exchange Clint certainly had not figured the men to be lawmen. Now, where he had once been curious about what happened, Clint was downright confused.

"So you recognized one of the marshals?" he asked.

The driver was finished with his unloading and climbed up into his seat to grab his reins.

"Yeah, I did. His name's Klellan." Chuckling, the driver wiped a layer of sweat from his forehead with his sleeve and regarded Clint with an amused expression. "Why all the questions? Did you think we was gettin' robbed back there?"

Clint laughed and said, "The thought had crossed my mind."

"Well, sorry 'bout that, friend, but it weren't nothin' of the sort. Ask that fella down there if we was robbed."

Clint turned around to see a skinny man in glasses and a brown suit lugging the stage's strongbox across the street to the bank. Next to him was an armed escort who kept a close eye on the street and everyone passing by. Sure enough, robbers would have made off with the box.

"Want me to take your horse along to the livery with my team?" the driver offered.

"No, I'll take him. Thanks anyway, though."

Clint untied Duke from the rear of the stage and watched as the coach rumbled off to the livery. He was surprised that it wasn't leaving little pieces of itself behind it.

As he patted the black gelding's snout, he started to feel the excitement growing once again. The clean mountain air smelled fresh and crisp. The streets of Denver bustled with life that seemed all the more energetic to him after having spent time in Cedar Cross.

Clint led Duke to the livery and passed the stage

driver, who was on his way to the nearest saloon. Inside the corral the man who had ridden shotgun was securing the coach and helping tend to the horses. Clint paid the stable boy for the next two days in advance and left, heading for a hotel.

Eager to see Jeanette after all this time, Clint thought he could hear her sultry voice whispering in his ear. He no longer cared about finding out about the marshals and Arlo Gentry. All Clint wanted was to put his hands around Jeanette's trim waist, bury his face in her hair, and feel her smooth body pressed to his.

They had a lot of catching up to do.

TEN

Del Thayer did a double take when he saw none other than Clint Adams walking across the street from the livery stable. After being in Denver for a few days now, not only had he spotted the man he'd been tracking, but he'd also stumbled upon an additional surprise.

Thayer knew Clint Adams on sight, having crossed paths with him several times before. Thayer clenched his fists, as if to keep his current target from slipping away. Already the man had lost himself in the maze of Denver's hotels and gambling halls. Clint, however, seemed to be going in the opposite direction.

Good, Thayer thought. I hope he stays away from me this time. He'd had nothing but bad luck in his past dealings with Clint Adams.

Thayer knew better than to get in Clint's way, but the bounty hunter needed to bag this target. Lately, the pickings had been slim and he was getting desperate for the kind of money that was being offered for this man's capture.

Keeping an eye on Clint while heading for a nearby casino, the bounty hunter couldn't help but feel an additional twinge of excitement at the thought of facing down Clint Adams. If that was what it came to, he'd do what needed to be done without a moment's hesitation.

Gunsmith or not, Thayer had seen Gentry first.

Clint got himself settled at the Denver House Hotel, where he usually stayed when he was in Denver. That done he tracked down the address Bill Henderschott had supplied him for Jeanette Colvin.

Situated between a barbershop and a newspaper office, the general store was recessed from the street and was obviously an older building. Instead of painted lettering on the wide, plate glass window of the storefront, a wooden sign resembling a doctor's shingle announced the name of the store: COLVIN'S DRY GOODS.

It wasn't much of a store. It seemed that Jeanette Colvin had fallen on hard times.

He entered the store, and the inside looked a little better. All the essentials seemed to be there, from boots to grain, each of the four aisles was stocked with everything a consumer could want or need. It wasn't until he reached the back of the store, however, that Clint found what *he* wanted.

Jeanette saw him the moment she stepped from behind a pile of blankets, and she jumped a little in surprise. Her lips were just the way Clint remembered them. The upper lip was thin and bow-shaped, the lower was fuller and ripe. They worked well together, he knew, especially when they formed the warm, generous smile that now graced her features.

"Clint, you came! I'm so happy you're here."

Smiling, Clint opened his arms and Jeanette bounded into them, smothering his face with kisses. She was five and a half feet tall and light in his grasp as he lifted her. The dark red dress she wore was simple but attractive, complementing the thick brown hair that flowed over her shoulders.

"As soon as I got the word that you were here I dropped everything to come and see you."

On her feet again she stepped back and quickly straightened her hair. The few customers in the place were looking on with interest as the store owner tried to regain her composure.

"Marshal Henderschott came through here a few days ago and I heard him say he was working with you. I asked him to pass along my message, but I never expected to see you so soon."

"I was running with one of Bill's posses when he told me."

She snaked her arm through his and said, "I'm so glad to see you. Will you be staying long?"

"A few days, at least."

"Good." She put her mouth near his ear. "I've missed you."

"When do you finish here?"

"I close at six," she said. "Why don't you pick me up then and we'll have dinner and . . . and catch up."

"I'll be here, Jeanette."

She gave him a quick kiss on the cheek and sent him on his way. As he was leaving he heard one of the customers, an elderly woman wrapped in a battered shawl, approach Jeanette and speak in an excited stage whisper.

"About time you found someone, child," she said. "He seems like a nice young man."

If only she knew what he had in mind for that "child," he thought.

And judging by the wicked smile on Jeanette's face, she was thinking the same thing.

ELEVEN

While Denver was much bigger than Cedar Cross, it still had all the elements catering to rugged men with gold in their pockets. Walking back to the Denver House, Clint could see the change in atmosphere from the quiet business area where Jeanette's store was located to the rowdier "entertainment district."

On the way to his hotel Clint saw something he had never seen before. Obviously it had opened since the last time he'd been here.

It was called the Mountaintop Poker Hall, and it attracted his attention immediately. He crossed the street and entered.

Along one side of the room was a large bar that looked solid, although it had plainly seen its fair share of hard times. No doubt, it had been imported from some other such place and had existed through all of this before, many times. It had the scars to prove it.

Behind the bar were two bartenders keeping all of the players and their companions sufficiently liquored up to keep losing their money to the house.

There were twenty felt-covered tables scattered around the room, with a game going on at each one. Most of the tables had four men seated at them, with an open seat. As Clint walked around he noticed that the higher stakes games were in the back. Circulating among the players were the ever present working girls, the establishment's last effort to relieve the gamblers of whatever money they had left.

Clint felt right at home in the loud, bustling atmosphere and walked straight to the bar to order a beer. With a mug in hand he started circulating himself, slower this time. He wandered among the tables, drawing an occasional glance from a player, observing the people who were playing, and the size of the pots involved.

He settled on a table where the men looked like they knew what they were doing but weren't playing for very big stakes. Neither were they playing penny ante. He was only looking to pass time, so he sat down. He put the beer down on the table, but he wouldn't finish it while he was gambling.

After the third hand Clint looked up from the table for a moment and noticed a familiar face across the room. Sitting at one of the tables farthest from the door and facing the bar, Arlo Gentry looked every bit as guarded and uncomfortable as he had on the stage from Cedar Cross.

Clint looked away as the cards for the next hand were dealt. What did he care about Gentry now? He relaxed and started to enjoy himself.

There he was again.

Laying low in a shadowy corner at the far end of the bar, Del Thayer felt a nervous tic pull at the corner of his right eye when he spotted Clint Adams at a poker table not too far from where Arlo Gentry was sitting.

"I'll be damned," Thayer muttered to himself.

He thought Clint Adams would have better things to do than horn in on his bounty. Pushing away from the bar Thayer walked toward Gentry's table. He walked straight over to his target and stuck his gun discreetly into the smaller man's side. He leaned over so he could whisper into his ear without the other players hearing him.

"Come along with me with no fuss, Gentry," he whispered. "You give me any trouble and you'll ride out of Denver draped over a saddle. The poster says dead or alive, so let's go."

None of the other players heard what he said, but they were watching Gentry, waiting for him to finish his business so they could get on with the game. Still wearing his poker face Gentry folded, swept his winnings into his hat, and got up to leave.

Without another word Thayer followed his prisoner out of the gaming hall and into the street. He'd wanted to move on Gentry with a little more privacy, but the sight of Clint Adams had changed his plan. He didn't want to take a chance on losing his bounty to the other man.

Despite the change, the whole thing had gone much smoother than he'd expected and Thayer smiled as he nudged Gentry along. Soon, he thought, they'd be mounted and on their way out of Denver.

After rounding a corner the bounty hunter could tell he was being followed. He slowed their progress and hissed at Gentry to stop, while pressing the barrel of his gun harder into the man's back. His hand went into his jacket and touched the smaller gun he kept there. He pushed Gentry into an alley and told him to keep quiet. With a quick glance behind them he saw who was on their tail.

"Ah, shit," he said, spotting Clint Adams about half a block behind them.

TWELVE

The blaring noise around Clint was a mixture of clinking glasses, squealing women, and boisterous gamblers that all but drowned out the piano player sitting in the corner with his back to the room. His cards were falling well, and Clint was thoroughly enjoying himself.

Every once in a while he would glance up from his hand to scan the other players and take a look around the room. Doing just that, Clint's eyes again fell upon Gentry's table and stayed there. More specifically, he was watching a tall, bulky man in a battered jacket, who was obviously hiding a gun in his right hand.

Nobody else seemed to notice. Too wrapped up in their own affairs, all of the gamblers and saloon girls stepped aside to let the armed man pass without so much as a look in his direction. Clint kept a close watch on that man as he made his way through the

46

crowd, heading straight for Gentry's table.

Whoever the man was, by the intense look on his stubble-covered face, the unwavering predator's eyes, and his serious mouth that formed a grim line across his face, he obviously meant business. In seconds he was at Gentry's table, whispering something into the man's ear.

Clint took his cards and held them in front of him without even looking at them. Still watching the scene a few tables away, he wanted to wait and see what was going to happen. He knew if the man with the jacket had wanted Gentry dead he could have shot him already. As it was, he seemed more interested in getting Gentry's attention without alerting the other card players.

Just as Clint expected, Gentry raked his money from the table and stood up stiffly. He walked to the door with the other man very close behind him. Clint watched intently, and as both men went through the door to the outside he took a quick look at his cards before throwing them down and pushing away from the table.

He'd been dealt an ace-high flush.

"Damn it," he said, sweeping his money of the table, "I fold."

After leaving the poker hall Clint spotted the gunman and Gentry walking down the street and followed. He didn't know what Gentry had that the other man wanted, but this was the second time he'd been plucked out of a group by some mystery man with a gun in his hand.

While he'd had his suspicions on the stagecoach, Clint was certain that Gentry's life was in danger this time. Also, he was very curious now to find out just what the hell was going on with the little man.

Giving them a small lead Clint decided to follow and not make a move until he had to. Unfortunately, the gunman must have spotted him because suddenly the man slowed, then stepped into a doorway or an alley. Clint stopped dead and waited. When the two men did not reappear he started forward again.

As Clint got closer he saw the mouth of the alley. Had they simply stepped into it to get away from him, or was there a way out?

As he turned into the alley he saw a flurry of motion. Apparently, the man with the gun had been so intent on him that Gentry had been able to get the drop on him. The small man whirled around, caught the gunman's wrist, twisted it, and relieved him of his gun. At the same time he pushed the man away from him, and then pointed his gun.

Clint still didn't know what was going on, but clearly Gentry was going to shoot the now unarmed man.

"Don't do it!" he shouted.

With that, Gentry turned and trained the gun on him. Clint had no time to think. Even he found it ironic as he drew that he was having to kill a man he thought he was going to help. He drew and fired before Gentry could pull the trigger. As the bullet struck Gentry, he reflexively pulled the trigger of his stolen gun and his shot pounded into the ground at his own feet.

The second man stood like a petrified statue, not daring to move until he saw what Clint was going to do.

Gentry staggered from the force of the shot, then dropped to the ground where he remained motionless.

Shifting his aim a few inches Clint covered the other man, whose hand was still inside his jacket.

"Take your hand out of your jacket real slowly, friend."

Thayer did as he was told and felt his stomach clench. Clint approached him and quickly relieved him of the second gun.

"What the hell's going on here?" a voice called out.

Both Clint and Thayer looked toward the entrance of the alley. A uniformed Denver policeman stood there with his own weapon out.

"Mister," he said, "I'd advise you to drop that gun."

"I'll holster it, Officer," Clint said, and did so. "But I shot this man in self-defense."

"It's true," Thayer was quick to add. "He also saved my life."

The policeman took in the scene and then seemed to relax. He also holstered his gun.

"I'm afraid I'll need you boys to come with me and make a statement."

"No problem," Clint said.

"Yes, sir," Thayer said. "It would be my pleasure."

"I'll have to get someone to clean up this mess," the policeman said.

Clint smiled and said, "We'll wait."

It took a couple of hours, but they were finally released by the police.

"I've got some questions for you," Clint said as he and Thayer left the station. "I recognize you now."

"Let me buy you a drink, Adams," Thayer said. "It's the least I can do for the man who saved my life."

"I'd sure like to know why I had to kill that man," Clint said.

"In here," Thayer said, indicating a saloon that was about a half a block from the police station. "We can talk in here."

THIRTEEN

Clint followed Del Thayer into the saloon without bothering to look at the name of the place. Both men quickly ordered their drinks and found a table in the back where they could talk privately.

"You're a bounty hunter," Clint said, "but I can't place you."

"No reason you should," Thayer said. "We only crossed paths once or twice. You were with those lady bounty hunters."

He was talking about Anne Archer, Sandy Spillane, and Katy Littlefeather, three remarkable women and partners who worked as bounty hunters.

"The name's Del Thayer."

Clint frowned. The man's face was familiar, but the name didn't ring any bells.

Thayer looked to be in his late thirties, stood just as tall as Clint but carried more weight. His hair was blond and shaggy beneath a black Stetson. His face

looked European, with sunken cheekbones that gave
him a menacing look and made his face memorable.
In the right light, he resembled a live corpse.

Sipping his beer Clint set the glass aside and
looked Thayer in the eyes.

"Now tell me why I had to kill Arlo Gentry,
Thayer," he said.

"To keep him from killing me, obviously," Thayer
said. "I was taking him in for the bounty on him,
Adams. That's all."

"He seems to have been pretty popular," Clint
said, "but who was he?"

Thayer looked surprised.

"You sayin' you don't know who he was?"

"Just his name."

"I thought you might be after him, yourself."

Clint shook his head.

"I'm not a bounty hunter," Clint explained, "never
have been. I'm just here to see an old friend. All Gentry was to me was another passenger on the stage
into town. Why don't you just tell me why you were
after him."

"Arlo Gentry robbed a Wells Fargo payroll last
month, shot down three guards and disappeared
with five thousand dollars. He's been on the run
since then, and the price on his head has gone up
every month he's been missing."

Pausing to finish his whiskey, Thayer seemed
more at ease in his seat and wiped his mouth with
the back of his hand before continuing.

"I caught up with him and some of his men last
week and waited for a chance to get him when he
was alone. The way things are around here with the
law I'm surprised I found him at all."

Clint had heard of the Wells Fargo robbery but had
only caught a description of the thieves with no
names to go by. Thinking back, Gentry did fit the
description of the gang's leader, a slightly built man

who looked like anything but a robber. Also, the man's behavior on the stagecoach perfectly fit that of a man on the run.

When the bounty hunter spoke about the law it triggered another memory for Clint.

"Does the name Klellan mean anything to you?"

"Marshal Klellan?"

"That's the one."

Now Thayer seemed evasive, his eyes darting around the room.

"Are you . . . friends with Klellan?"

"I don't know him," Clint said.

Thayer seemed relieved by that.

"Klellan is the main reason I almost gave up on catching Gentry without getting shot or hanged, myself."

"What do you mean?"

"He's as crooked as a sidewinder, Adams, and every bit as dangerous—and he's not the only one."

Thayer waved to the bartender, and the scrawny man brought over another beer and whiskey. After downing the liquor the bounty hunter cleared his throat.

"Why did you ask about Klellan?" he asked Clint.

Clint proceeded to tell the man about what he'd seen when the stage was stopped by two men and Gentry was called out by the two men on horseback.

"The bag Gentry handed over," Thayer said. "Was it a brown, heavy carpetbag?"

"That's the one."

"That explains why Gentry didn't put up much of a fight earlier. That bag held all the money he robbed from Wells Fargo."

"Why would Marshal Klellan take the money and not Gentry?"

"He took the money for himself, Adams. I told ya, he's crooked. I'm sure he stopped that coach to give Gentry a choice. Either hand the money over and keep quiet about it, or be arrested. It's happening all over the Rockies. The law's for sale hereabouts."

Clint's eyes narrowed as all the pieces fell into place. As much as he didn't want to believe Thayer, the man's story fit with all the facts. The hairs on the back of Clint's neck raised up, and he could feel the anger boiling in his stomach. More than anything, he hated dishonest lawmen. Although he'd worn a badge years and years ago, many of his friends were lawmen.

"You mentioned that Klellan wasn't the only one involved," Clint said. "Who else is there?"

Thayer shrugged and shook his head. "Hell if I know. What I do know is that whoever they are, they're becoming rich men. For months now, all I hear from every piece of dirt I catch up with is that the law's for sale in these parts for whoever has enough money—and enough money can buy them out of any charge."

"Even murder?"

Thayer shrugged.

"Gentry killed three men during that robbery," he said. "You figure it out."

"What about the local law? They crooked, too?"

"I'm not sure," Thayer said. "Denver's got a police department. That might be different. Anyway, I'm cutting my losses and heading somewhere else, somewhere the law's still honest."

It was getting close to six o'clock now and Clint didn't want to be late for his appointment with Jeanette. On the other hand, he was starting to feel bad about robbing Thayer of his bounty—indirectly.

"I'm sorry about Gentry," Clint said. "The price on his head must have been pretty high."

"Yeah, it was."

"I'm sorry I cost you that money."

"Well, maybe you didn't."

"What do you mean?"

"Well . . . you killed him. You could collect the bounty and we could split it."

"I don't want money for killing Gentry."

Thayer sat back in his chair, dejected.

"You can have it," Clint said.

"What?"

"I'll talk to the police and have them pay you," Clint said. "If I don't want the money, what else can they do?"

"They can keep it themselves, if they're crooked."

"Well," Clint said, "I guess there's only one way to find out."

FOURTEEN

As Clint approached Colvin's Dry Goods he could see the owner waiting just inside the door, holding a wooden sign that said CLOSED.

Testing the front door he found it unlocked and stuck his head inside.

"Is it all right for me to come in?"

"Of course. I was just finishing up here and then we can get some supper."

Clint stepped inside the empty store and looked around. Although the place looked the same, it felt different without the browsing customers. Jeanette seemed more at ease now that they were alone in the store.

"I've been waiting a long time to see you," Clint said, eyeing her appreciatively. There was a fine sheen of sweat on her brow that did nothing to diminish her beauty. In fact, it caused him to wonder where else there might be some perspiration gathered.

With all the events of the day he'd almost forgotten why he was in Denver in the first place. Seeing Jeanette's body twisting and stretching beneath her dress he suddenly ached to be close to her.

Jeanette knew he was watching her as she straightened her stock, working her way to the back of the store.

"This has been a long day for me, too," she said, turning to face him. "How about this? I'll finish straightening later. I'll just count the money and then we can work up an appetite for supper."

He reached for her and said, "How about this, instead?"

He pulled her to him and kissed her deeply. She pressed herself tightly to him and her lips parted, allowing her tongue to probe his mouth.

The kiss continued for what seemed like forever, but eventually she pulled away and walked toward a doorway at the back of the room. Clint followed and found her waiting in a dark, cramped supply room, already tugging at the ribbons holding the front of her dress together.

"It's not a hotel suite, but I can't wait any longer," she said as the thin cotton material dropped to the floor. Pulling Clint's shirt open, she ran her hands over his chest.

"I need you right now," she whispered, "before I explode."

Clint was quickly out of his clothes, and Jeanette took her hands off of him just long enough to peel away the few undergarments she wore.

Standing naked in front of him, she looked as though she were about to burst. Her breasts were rounded and firm, and trembled slightly with every breath she took. Beads of perspiration ran down from between her breasts to her taut tummy.

"I need a bath . . ." she said.

"You're fine," he said, "just fine . . ."

Most of her dark hair was flowing down her back, but a few stray wisps spilled onto her chest and the ends tickled her small, pink nipples.

Clint's bare skin felt none of the cool air around him as Jeanette's warm, moist flesh pressed tightly against his own. What his eyes were denied by the dark he made up for with his hands as he reached for her and ran them over her body, cupping her breasts, flicking the nipples with his thumbs, running his hands over her belly and then around behind her to hold her firm buttocks.

Jeanette moaned slightly at his touch and ground her hips against him, trapping his stiffened penis between them.

He could feel her wetness, and smell it. She was ready for him. There was nowhere to lie down, but that did not deter them for a moment. Clint lifted her up and set her down again onto a waist-high stack of crates covered with a burlap sack.

Jeanette reached for his cock, stroking it as her mouth worked eagerly over his neck and shoulders. Clint pushed her back and reached for her breasts again, able to see them now that his eyes were adjusting to the dark.

He stroked her breasts, then leaned forward to kiss them, sucking the nipples into his mouth. He went to his knees as he kissed her belly, licking the sweat from her, working his way down until he was between her legs. He spread her legs and settled them onto his shoulders so that she was wide open for him. He leaned forward and began to kiss her gently, licking her, touching her, working her into a frenzy until finally his tongue touched that magic spot and her hips began to twitch uncontrollably.

He stood quickly, before the sensations could fade, and guided himself into the steamy depth of her. She tried to close her legs around him, but he grasped her firmly by the ankles and spread her even wider, driving himself in and out of her mindlessly. Finally he exploded inside of her with a loud groan, and she laughed with pleasure and held him close until his tremor subsided.

"Now that," she said in his ear, "was worth waiting for!"

FIFTEEN

For the rest of the evening Clint was with Jeanette, who took him to most of her favorite spots around Denver. He had been in Denver many times before, but he allowed her to be his guide, since the city was fairly new to her. When they wound up back in Clint's room at the Denver House, under the soft quilt with the moonlight coming in the window, they both felt they had found the best spot in town.

The next morning she awoke first and slipped out from under the covers to pull on her cotton dress. Clint opened his eyes in time to watch.

"I thought you'd want to work up an appetite for breakfast before you left," he said.

Jeanette smiled at him and bent down to kiss him.

"My store is supposed to open in an hour, and I've got to get bathed and changed before someone sees me in this dress for a second day in a row. I'll eat something at the store."

It was early and Clint was still tired. After Jeanette waved good-bye and slipped out the door, he rolled over to get a few minutes more rest. He awoke for the second time feeling refreshed and rejuvenated. He got dressed and went downstairs for a good breakfast in the Denver House's fine dining room.

Clint and Thayer had arranged to meet in the morning back at the police station where they'd made their statements. He found Thayer already there, in the office of a Lieutenant Wilkins, along with the policeman who had brought them in, Officer Clontz. Clontz was a smooth-faced man in his twenties, while Wilkins had muttonchops and was in his early forties.

"Mr. Adams?" the lieutenant said, standing up from his desk.

"That's right."

The two men shook hands.

"Please, sit down. I've already read your statements and heard what Mr. Thayer had to say about the, uh, incident yesterday. Perhaps you'd tell me your side?"

Briefly, Clint explained how he had seen the two men leaving the poker hall and decided to follow.

"Let me interrupt you here, if I may?"

"Of course."

"Why did you follow?"

"It looked like trouble was brewing."

"For whom?"

"I couldn't tell that," Clint said.

"Why would you become involved in someone else's trouble?"

Clint shrugged.

"It's a bad habit I have that I can't break."

"All right, then," Wilkins said, "continue."

Clint explained that curiosity and suspicion had

brought him to that alley. Quick thinking and re-
flexes caused him to leave it alive. What he didn't
mention was what he and Thayer had talked about
in the saloon afterward.

Lieutenant Wilkins nodded silently as Clint spoke,
and did not interrupt again.

"Your story checks out with what Mr. Thayer told
us," Wilkins said when Clint was finished. "I don't
see any problem with writing this off as self-
defense."

"I'm glad to hear that, Lieutenant."

"You fellows are free to go."

Thayer looked at Clint, who knew what he was
thinking.

"There's one more thing, Lieutenant."

"What's that?"

"There's the matter of the bounty on Gentry's
head."

Wilkins sat back in his chair.

"I'm aware of your background, Adams, but I
wasn't aware that you were a bounty hunter now."

"I'm not," Clint said. "I was thinking that I wanted
the bounty to go to Thayer."

Wilkins frowned.

"I can authorize the bounty to be paid to you," he
said, "and then what you do with it is your business.
Will that suit you?"

"That's fine," Clint said.

"It'll take a day or two, I suspect," Wilkins said.
"Where are you staying?"

"The Denver House."

Wilkins nodded.

"Fine hotel."

"Yes, it is."

"I'll send word to you when your money is available."

"That's fine."

Clint wondered how he could bring up the subject

of law for sale without offending anyone.

"Is there something else?"

"Just some rumors I've been hearing."

"About what?"

"Well . . . I've heard stories about men like Gentry buying their way out of custody."

Wilkins's frown deepened.

"I've heard those rumors myself," he said. "Every piece of scum I lock up has heard them, too. They're real surprised when I throw their bribes back in their faces." He leaned forward now. "You weren't thinking that I might be for sale, too, were you?"

"To be honest, Lieutenant," Clint said, "I don't know what to think. I'm just bothered by the rumors."

"So am I," Wilkins said, "and I'm bothered by the fact that they might be true. If I run across a crooked lawman, though, I'll throw him into a cell as fast as I would any lawbreaker."

"I'm glad to hear you say that, Lieutenant."

"Your bounty money is safe, Adams," Wilkins said in a tone of voice that Clint didn't like. It seemed that the lieutenant didn't quite believe that he wasn't in this for the money.

"I trust it is, Lieutenant," Clint said. "Thanks for your time and understanding."

"Sure."

Wilkins made no move to shake hands with either man as Clint and Thayer both left.

SIXTEEN

Spending the next two days in the Mountaintop
Poker Hall, and the nights with Jeanette Colvin, Clint
allowed the incident with Gentry and Del Thayer to
fade away—as much as the memory of killing a man
can fade away. In Jeanette's arms he found it easy
to believe there was nothing else in town besides her
and the down quilt of his room at the Denver House.

Gentry's body went unclaimed and eventually was
put in the ground with a simple wooden cross to
mark the spot.

On the second day Clint received word that the
money was ready. He went and got it and turned it
over to Del Thayer. Not wanting to risk losing it,
Thayer left Denver that same day and headed east,
looking for "legal law," as he called it.

Clint decided not to spend any more time thinking
about dirty lawmen. He decided to enjoy Jeanette
and let the law clean its own house.

Lying in the modest bed over Colvin's Dry Goods, Clint held Jeanette in his arms and closed his eyes as she ran her fingernails over his chest. The scent of their lovemaking still hung in the air, mixing with that of her hair and skin. It smelled sweet and Clint found himself happy and content.

"I think I need a vacation," Jeanette said, breaking the blissful silence.

Clint opened his eyes and found her staring at him.

"Has it been so bad that you're thinking about getting away from me?" he asked.

Smacking him playfully, Jeanette rolled over on top of him, allowing her hair to spill over her shoulders and her nipples to brush his chest.

"That's not what I meant and you know it. I mean I want to get away from everything except you."

"Isn't your business fairly new?"

"This one is," she said, "but I've been trying to make businesses run successfully for years, and this one just might make it. I don't know how much longer you'll be in town, but I want to enjoy you while you're here."

"Can you get someone to take over, so you don't have to close?"

"Maybe," she said. "I'll have to look into it."

As she spoke she squirmed on top of him, massaging his crotch with the warmth between her legs. Even though his body was responding to her Clint did no more than knead her smooth buttocks and lightly kiss her perfumed neck. He wanted to give her the time to talk.

"If it works out we don't have to stay here. How about San Francisco?" he asked. "That's a city we could get lost in for a while."

"Too expensive," she said as she arched her back and stroked his belly with her fingertips.

"Dallas, then. Or maybe New Orleans."

"Too far."

Clint was getting frustrated that his suggestions weren't acceptable.

"I heard there's some real poker action going on in Leadville, and that's only a commuter train away," he said, only half seriously.

Jeanette's face brightened and she beamed down at him.

"Now that's more like it. That's not far at all, but far enough to get away from it all."

"You're kidding."

"Why?"

"Leadville is pretty tough. I thought you'd want something more fancy."

"I just want to get away," she said. "It doesn't have to be fancy, as long as we're together."

"But a mining camp—"

"Can we go, please? I think it would be interesting."

"Well," he said, "I probably know some people there—"

But before he could say another word Jeanette took his mind away from travel plans by rubbing her breasts over him, first his chest, then his belly, and then she was rolling his rigid cock between them, flicking her tongue out at it now and then before finally taking him into her warm, wet mouth.

"Leadville it is," Clint groaned.

SEVENTEEN

The next morning Clint and Jeanette took their time getting dressed and went to Clint's hotel for breakfast. Afterward Clint walked her out to the street. It was going to be another clear, cool day, and Clint was suddenly glad that they weren't leaving Colorado for their trip.

"You check on the train schedule and pack your things," Jeanette said, "and I'll spend the day straightening everything at my store."

"See you tonight."

After she left, Clint remained outside to fill his lungs with the crisp mountain air. The wind felt cleaner here and the air seemed lighter and more pure than it did anywhere else. People came to Colorado to feel better, he knew.

Sick people had chosen this area as a place to ease the tensions on their hearts and lungs. Now he knew why. It was beautiful and, although he had nothing at all wrong with him, Clint felt better, too.

He took a brisk walk to the train station and checked the schedule on the wall. The next commuter train to Leadville was at eleven a.m. the next morning. He bought two tickets.

The train pulled into the station at two minutes past eleven, with Clint and Jeanette waiting for it on a platform that still smelled of fresh pines. Their bags were loaded into the front of the third passenger car by a conductor who also examined their tickets. The ride to Leadville would be a short one and the train was filled with commuters, most of whom were businessmen.

Clint took a seat in the car's middle row next to Jeanette as the train lurched to a noisy start. The whistle blew and the steam pushed the engine forward, taking them down the tracks and away from Denver.

Inside, the other passengers created a busy commotion that made conversation almost impossible. Couples on either side of Clint were chatting loudly, a baby cried in its mother's arms, a man in the rear of the car coughed loudly and liquidly, and a fat old-timer snored behind Jeanette's seat. None of this mattered, however, because both were excited to be on their way.

Jeanette filled the time by talking in Clint's ear, filling him in on what she'd been doing before he arrived in Denver. Since the last time he saw her Clint had had more than his fill of good and bad times, but rather than dwell on all of that he simply nodded and let Jeanette tell her own story.

All the while, his attention was divided between her and the loud activity around them. By the time they were an hour into their journey, the baby had stopped crying and most of the other conversations had died down to snores and quiet voices. However, the man in the back of the car still had his periodic bouts of coughing that trailed off to a dry, labored wheezing.

Something about the sound struck a chord in Clint's mind and he turned on his hard, wooden seat to get a better look.

"What's the matter?" Jeanette asked. "Am I talking too much?"

Clint scanned the back of the car, looking for the owner of the hacking cough.

"No, it's not you. I thought I heard something familiar, that's all."

"You know so many people, it wouldn't surprise me if you stumbled across some long lost friend on this very train."

Curious, she turned around to look where Clint was staring, but she saw nothing out of the ordinary. Just before both of them gave up on their visual search a large, old man with a body resembling a tree trunk shifted in his seat and turned to lean against the window for some shut-eye. In doing so he made it possible for Jeanette to see the last seat in the car, which had previously been hidden from view.

Her eyes widened when she saw who was sitting there.

"Do you know who that is?" she whispered to Clint.

Clint nodded as the memories came rushing back to him.

"I sure do," he said, staring at the pale, sunken face of John Henry "Doc" Holliday. "We've met on a few occasions."

Checking his pocket watch Clint saw that they had plenty of time before pulling into Leadville. He started to get up from his seat but paused to look at Jeanette.

"How do you know Doc?" he asked curiously.

Shrugging, Jeanette said, "He comes into Denver whenever there's a big game in town. He doesn't cause much trouble, but he's still a very well-known man."

"Why don't you stay put while I go talk to Doc for a little while. I have some questions that he might be able to answer for me."

"Yes, sir," she said and saluted.

EIGHTEEN

The last time Clint had seen Doc Holliday was in Tombstone, Arizona. There, Doc and Clint's friend Wyatt Earp had been knee-deep in a feud with a gang of rustlers led by the Clantons and the McLaurys. The whole situation had exploded into the now famous O.K. Corral shoot-out, and two of Wyatt's brothers had been gunned down in the aftermath. One of them was dead, one crippled, and Clint hadn't seen Wyatt since.

Doc hadn't looked good in Tombstone, but he'd looked better than he did now, slumped over in the last seat on the train to Leadville.

Spotting Clint as he walked down the aisle toward him, Doc instantly recognized him and started to say something, but he was cut off by another wracking coughing fit. He'd been plagued with consumption for years, and the bloody hacking had become a common trait to all who knew him.

When Clint sat down next to Doc he saw the sickly Georgian was wearing his usual black suit and string tie. Doc's cane lay on the floor at his feet next to a black hat that reminded Clint of something a plantation owner might wear. Looking bone-white and too thin, Doc's face still had a determined spark of life in it and the handshake he offered was stronger than Clint remembered.

Having lived the first part of his life as a dentist in Georgia, Doc could never stay out of trouble and soon took to the life of a professional gambler. When he discovered his life-threatening illness, he'd moved west in the hopes that the drier climate would ease the strain on his failing lungs. Whether it was the air or the continual flow of liquor he poured into his body that kept him alive, Doc didn't care. He'd accepted his inevitable death long ago and didn't much care how it came about.

Through the years he'd lived dangerously in the roughest parts of whatever town he happened to be in. Taking the rough path throughout life, Doc had acquired more than enough skill with a gun to become one of the deadliest shots Clint had ever known. While Clint didn't much care for Doc or his low regard for life, he couldn't help but respect the man for riding and living hard and spitting into the face of death every chance he got when it would have been so easy to simply have checked into a sanatorium and died.

Also, they had one thing in common. Both men counted Wyatt Earp among their closest friends. Wyatt was Doc's only true friend and Doc would have done anything for him . . . even if that meant hunting down and killing the men who had shot Wyatt's brothers.

"Hello, Doc," Clint said as he took a seat.

"Why, if it isn't the illustrious Clint Adams," Doc

said with a slight southern drawl. "What evah brings you to Leadville?"

"Just visiting. I heard you had some trouble in Tombstone before you left." Clint paused, knowing that Doc had been fond of Morgan Earp, who had been killed in retribution for the O.K. Corral incident. "I was very sorry to hear about Morg. He was a fine man."

"Yes," Doc said softly, "a damned shame to lose that boy."

There was an intensity in Doc's eyes that gave away the killer who lurked beneath his frail exterior.

After a moment of silence Doc coughed once into a white handkerchief and took a deep, ragged breath.

"You were nevah much for small talk, Adams," Doc said. "What's on your mind?"

"You know Wyatt better than anyone, Doc," Clint said. "I haven't heard from him in a while. I thought you might know how he was."

Doc looked over at Clint, unable to hide his suspicion. When it came to Wyatt Earp he was very protective. Ever since the men responsible for the shooting of Morg and Virgil Earp had started dropping like flies, Wyatt had been a wanted man. Doc, himself, was on the top of a few of the law's wanted lists.

"Who are you workin' for, Adams?" Doc asked. "I thought you were Wyatt's friend."

"It's not like that, Doc," Clint said. "I just want to know if he's all right. Hell, I can understand how he feels after all that's happened. He is my friend, though, and I'm concerned for him."

After considering what Clint had said, Doc spoke, though his lips barely seemed to move underneath his bushy mustache. "He's just fine. Now, considah this subject closed."

Other questions concerning Wyatt Earp still hung in Clint's mind, but he let them rest for the moment.

"So, what business do you have in Leadville, Doc? Is Kate with you?"

"Leadville is where the money is, for the moment," Doc said. "And Kate is happily absent, for now. I'd probably sleep bettah if she stayed that way."

Big Nose Kate Elder was the whore who traveled with Doc and was the closest thing to a wife he'd had for several years. On more than one occasion, however, she had proven herself to be more trouble than she was worth. To say the least, Doc and Kate's relationship was stormy, but they usually managed to stay together. It was a match made in hell.

"Seems Leadville has some high-stakes poker games going, and plenty of players are coming for their share."

"Save the pitch, Adams," Doc said. "I'm already sold."

Leaning forward Doc glanced at the seat several rows in front of him at the back of Jeanette's head.

"Looks like your friend's gettin' lonely," he said. "Why don't you leave me to my peace and quiet while you see to your lovely companion."

"We're both headed for the same place, Doc," Clint said. "I'll be seeing you later. Try to stay out of trouble. Maybe I'll catch up to you for a drink so we can continue our discussion."

Clearing his throat in a painful-sounding rumble, Doc leaned back and closed his eyes.

"I'll be counting the moments," he said.

Clint headed back to where Jeanette was sitting and thought back briefly to the time he and Doc had crossed paths before. On one or two of those occasions he had come close to actually liking Doc Holliday.

This time, however, was not one of them.

NINETEEN

When the train pulled into Leadville, everyone in Clint's car got up to leave. They all grabbed their bags from the front compartment next to the door and filed out into the cold, breezy air that was dirtied with coal smoke and steam. Jeanette had a hotel already picked out that was one of the nicer ones in town according to one of her regular customers.

Looking over his shoulder before stepping down to the platform, Clint noticed that Doc was hanging back, probably to make sure he was the last one off the train. Although he fancied himself a gambler first and foremost, Doc had all the instincts and paranoia of a professional gunman. From what Clint had seen, Doc was one of the fastest draws there ever was—with the definite exception of Wild Bill.

"Come on, Clint," Jeanette said. "Forget about him for now. Let's get our room so we can start relaxing."

Turning back toward Jeanette, Clint said, "You're

right. I'd rather keep my eye on you, anyway."

Besides, he thought, a man like Doc Holliday shouldn't be too hard to find in any gambling town. And for the time being Leadville was *the* gambling town.

Compared to Denver, Leadville was obviously much smaller. On the short walk from the train station to the Four Star Hotel, Clint could feel a different kind of energy pulsing through Leadville's streets. It was the same kind of energy flowing through every town chosen by the nation's gamblers as the current hot spot.

For a while it had been Dodge City. Then came Cheyenne. Fort Wagner, Texas, had its moment in the sun, and Leadville had been there once, and was now again. All of the major cities and quite a few small towns had their time in the spotlight as the host to high-stakes poker games attended by the biggest gamblers around.

Clint loved the feel of a "money town" and was growing more and more anxious to find a place to sit down and start playing. Jeanette, on the other hand, had her own ideas.

"I say we stay in tonight and entertain each other," she said, after they had checked into their suite at the Four Star. "Traveling all day just makes me feel . . . filthy."

Before Clint could answer she was out of her denim dress and crawling naked on the bed like a tawny cat. As much as he wanted to explore what Leadville had to offer, what Jeanette had to offer was just too hard to pass up. In moments, he was out of his clothes, as well, and behind her on the bed.

Her ass was firm and warm in his hands as she crawled forward to clutch the overstuffed pillows. Clint ran his fingers along her back as Jeanette arched her butt into the air, nestling against his stiffening cock. Leaning forward to caress her breasts as they swung freely over the down comforter, Clint found her nipples already erect, and she gave a little moan as he pinched them gently.

His rigid pole was rubbing between Jeanette's legs, where she was moist and ready for him. She turned to look at Clint over her shoulder, through her long, tousled hair as he reached down to guide himself into her. It felt as though he plunged deeper into her than he ever had before, and when his belly pushed against her soft, rounded ass she made a noise like a deep rumbling from the back of her throat.

Clint loved the way her back sloped down to her hips and back up to her neck. No longer watching him, Jeanette clawed at the headboard and shook her hair from side to side as Clint pounded her harder and faster.

When his passions came to their peak he dug his fingers deeper into her hips as her body clenched around him like a hot fist. Collapsing on the bed next to her, Clint took a deep breath and watched as Jeanette straightened up on her knees and looked down at him.

Absently, she ran her hands along her own body, slowly wiping away the fine layer of sweat that had covered her almost perfectly rounded breasts. Her touch continued over the slight contours of her stomach and down to where the thick patch of dark hair started to form.

Yeah, Clint thought as his body started to respond as though Jeanette were touching him rather than herself; poker can wait for a while longer.

Doc watched Clint get off the train and walk through the station with the slender brunette at his side. Wyatt had always said that Clint would be able to find a good-looking woman in a monastery. She was a little skinny for Doc's taste but pretty all the same.

Stepping out onto the train station platform and away from the smoke and noise that accompanied a locomotive, Doc coughed again into his handkerchief. For the last few days, his disease had been getting the better of him and he'd been laying low in a small Denver hotel. But the poker tables had been calling to him and, after all, the money was here and not in some sick bed.

Clint and his companion had disappeared down another street, but Doc didn't much care. He knew the man well enough by his reputation alone, and where the rumors stopped Wyatt Earp had told him the rest. To Doc, Clint was an acquaintance and nothing more. Hopefully, the man would stay out of his way.

Tucking away his handkerchief, Doc began walking, leaning on his cane. He'd always carried a cane when his consumption was giving him more trouble than usual, and this was one of the days it was needed the most. Days like these seemed to be growing in number, but that still didn't impede Doc's plan.

He only carried one bag, which he took straight to the Gold Strike Saloon, where he intended to spend most of his time.

"Evenin', Doc," Kit Farrell said from behind the long plank-board bar. Farrell owned the battered establishment and was preparing for another busy night.

Doc coughed in response as he wove his way between the card tables set up in front of a stage with holes big enough to swallow up any dancer who set foot on it. Stopping in front of where Farrell stood, Doc leaned on his cane and hacked violently into his white handkerchief.

"Same room as always?" Farrell asked.

"If you please, Kit," Doc said. "But first hand me down one of those bottles so I can satisfy the thirst of a weary traveler."

Kit placed a bottle of whiskey in front of Doc along with a rusted key. Shaking his head Doc took a healthy swig from the bottle.

"Where's Kate?" Farrell asked.

Doc didn't flinch as the mouthful of liquor burned its way down his throat.

"As long as she stays out of earshot, I could care less. You haven't seen her, have you?"

"Not since the last time you were here. What brings you to town, anyway?"

"Ah'm a sportin' man, Kit," Doc said, "you know that." He paused to take another healthy pull from the bottle. "Man's got to earn a living."

The liquor seemed to put some more wind back into Doc's sails, and he tucked the walking stick under his arm as he headed toward the upstairs rooms with the bottle clutched in one fist and his suitcase in the other. Before climbing to the second floor, Doc motioned for Farrell to come closer.

Doc leaned in so he couldn't be heard by the few other customers seated at tables near the stairs.

"Ah may be gettin' some visitors . . . the kind that wear a badge. Do me a favor and let me know who's lookin' before they find me." He slipped a folded bill into Kit's hand.

"Sure thing, Doc."

"One more thing. If Creek Johnson shows up, make sure I see him right away. Creek and I have some business to take care of."

As Doc's mustache curled above a wicked grin, Farrell nodded and went back to his post behind the bar. He liked Doc, sure enough, but there was something about the man that always made him more than a little nervous. Watching Doc climb up to his regular room, that feeling found its way back into the pit of Kit's stomach.

TWENTY

It wasn't until five o'clock the next evening when Clint had the energy or the desire to leave the hotel. For the last thirty-six hours he and Jeanette had been eating room service and enjoying the various comforts to be found inside their suite overlooking Tenth Street.

"I'm just going to stretch my legs for a few hours," Clint said.

Jeanette, slipping into one of her simple-looking dresses, threw Clint a playful look over her shoulder.

"I've got some business here, too. Besides, there's plenty of men out there who won't tire out so quickly."

When Clint stopped to stare back at her, she laughed and said, "Don't worry. A few of my suppliers are based in Leadville and I'm going to have a word with them. Go have fun, win some money, and I'll catch up to you later."

"I'll make sure to be back for dinner," Clint said.
"I'd like to have a meal at a real table tonight. Room
service tends to get old pretty quickly."

She rushed over to Clint and gave him a quick kiss
on the mouth before he turned and headed out of the
room and down the stairs.

According to the kid at the desk the closest places
to find a high-stakes poker game were on Thirteenth
Street. There he could find Hyman's as well as the
saloon owned by Bill Allen, who was also Leadville's
chief of police.

"Which would you recommend?" Clint asked.

"Well, Chief Allen runs a nice place, and both seem
about the same size. But most of the real gamblers
have been leaning toward Hyman's saloon."

"Why's that?"

The kid, who looked no more than seventeen with
a pockmarked face and a head full of red hair, appeared surprised that anyone would have to ask that
question.

"They know Doc's there, of course."

Clint had all but forgotten about Doc since he last
saw the skinny dentist on the train from Denver.

"That's where Doc Holliday plays?"

"Sure, he plays there. Deals faro, too. Folks say
he's a cold killer, but there ain't been no trouble from
him. Chief Allen says he wants to bring Doc in, but
I think he just wants a known man in his jail."

Clint had to laugh at this kid, who seemed filled
with more current events than the newspaper he'd
found folded in front of his door that morning.

"How do you know so much, kid?"

"My pa works for the paper here in town. *The
Democrat*. Writes the editorials."

"Well, I guess that explains it, then. Here you go."
Clint flipped a dollar to the boy, who deftly caught it
while it was still flipping in the air. "Thanks for the
tip. I may need some more advice from you later on."

"Be my pleasure, Mr. Adams."

"So you know who I am, too?"

"Sure do," the kid said. "You're as famous as Doc."

"Well, here's another dollar," Clint said, this time putting it right in the boy's hand.

"What's this for?"

"This is so you don't talk about me to people the way you talk about Doc," Clint said. "And if I hear that you are, I'll be back to collect that second dollar from you. Understand?"

The kid swallowed and said, "Sure thing, Mr. Adams. You can count on me."

"I knew I could."

Clint walked out and headed toward Thirteenth Street. Besides playing poker, he decided to do a few other things, as well. First, he'd check in with Chief of Police Bill Allen, let the man know he was in Leadville, and take the opportunity to size him up. If anyone could make money as a crooked lawman, it would be the chief of police of a town like Leadville.

Bill Allen looked more the part of a saloon owner and brawler than he did the chief of police. Standing Clint's height and wearing a white shirt with a badge pinned to the right pocket, Allen wore his gun just as plainly as the scowl on his face. When Clint walked in, he could tell that Allen's was definitely not the most popular place in town.

"Good evenin', there," Allen said as he walked between the poker tables. Only half of them were full, but the mountains of chips in front of the players told Clint that whatever customers Allen had, they had more than enough money to keep him happy.

Clint stood just inside the doorway and looked around. The gaming tables were on a section of the floor that was raised a foot higher than the rest. The place was large and seemed to be doing all right, despite the fact that it wasn't full.

The only other person in the saloon besides the owner to notice Clint's arrival was the bartender, who looked eager for someone to talk to. At a second glance, Clint realized there were more people there than he'd originally thought. It might have been half full, but given the size of the place, half was plenty.

"I said good evenin', friend," Allen said as he got closer to where Clint was standing.

This time Clint returned Allen's look and gave a nod in return.

"Evening, Chief."

"Are you new in town? I don't recall seeing you here before."

"Just arrived yesterday."

"You picked a good place to spend your time. I've got the most tables and the best liquor in Leadville— and my tables are honest." Allen sounded more like a snake oil salesman than a city official. "The night's just gettin' started. There are plenty of chairs available."

"Actually, I came by to talk to you in your, uh, official capacity . . . if you have some time?"

Allen sized Clint up with a quick head-to-toe glance.

"Sure," he said. "Step over to the bar."

Clint ordered a beer and Allen had the same. Both men took a few healthy swallows of their drinks before Clint broke the ice.

"My name is Clint Adams."

No reaction from Allen.

"I always like to check in with the authorities when I get into town because sometimes a reputation can make people nervous."

"Oh, I know who you are, Mr. Adams," Allen said. "You've been to Leadville before, before my time."

"Not for a while."

"What brings you here this time?"

"I'm here with a friend." Clint paused to take an-

other sip of his beer. It was honestly the best he had
tasted in quite a while. "I hear Doc Holliday is dealing
faro here in Leadville, as well. I've been told he can
be trouble."

That struck a chord with Allen.

"Holliday's a killer and a card cheat, but he's been
laying low. I know he's still wanted in Arizona, and
I'd be more than happy to put him out of circulation."

"Sounds personal to me," Clint said, as another
beer was placed in front of him. "What do you have
against Doc?"

"Nothing more than any other lawman. He's got
no respect for a badge, that's no secret, but I'll bring
him in, one way or another."

Allen's temper seemed to go up a few degrees the
more he thought about Doc, causing his face to twist
into an angry scowl.

"He's even trying to lie his way out of paying me
a gambling debt. The sick little weasel is no good use
to anyone as far as I can tell."

"Except maybe Wyatt Earp."

Now the look on Allen's face was one of puzzle-
ment.

"Now there's a relationship I'll never understand.
Earp is supposed to be a good lawman. What's he
doin' being friends with a man like Holliday?"

"A man's got the right to pick his own friends,"
Clint said.

"Are you friends with Doc?" Allen asked. "Is that
what you're trying to say?" His tone was belligerent.

"I'm friends with Wyatt," Clint said. "Doc and I are
more . . . acquaintances."

"Well," Allen said, "I got a right to my opinion, too,
and I say he's a liar and a cheat, and probably a cow-
ard, too."

"That's something I've never heard him accused
of," Clint said. "But speaking of liars I've been hear-

ing some rumors around Denver I was hoping to check out with you."

Allen seemed to have a different expression for every subject, but Clint had a hard time deciphering this one.

"Is this about those law for sale rumors?"

"Yes, it is."

"Yeah, I've heard those rumors, sure enough. I don't know how they run things in Denver, but things are on the up-and-up here in Leadville. Now, if you'll excuse me, I've got a business to run. Enjoy your stay."

Allen abruptly turned and left Clint standing there, causing Clint to wonder if the subject of crooked lawmen made Allen nervous.

Even though he'd been watching the man carefully for any kind of giveaway of an unintentional clue from the man's manner, Clint had still come up empty. It was obvious Bill Allen was a poker player as well as chief of police, because Clint wasn't quite sure what kind of hand the man was holding.

Full house or bluff?

Straight or crooked?

It was too early to decide, but Clint did decide that he'd watch Allen's tables for a while before sitting down to play. He'd be able to tell after a short time whether Allen was telling the truth about his tables being honest.

And if he'd lie about that, he'd lie about anything.

TWENTY-ONE

Hyman's was smaller than Bill Allen's saloon, but every inch of space available was occupied and the air was alive with rowdy laughter and an off-key piano being played in the back of the room. Along one entire side of the narrow room was an oak bar covered with mugs, bottles, and the occasional passed-out cowboy.

The other half of the place was filled with two rows of tables. The row closest to the bar was for poker games, while the row against the opposite wall was for blackjack, roulette, and faro. The moment Clint walked in, he felt more at ease than he had next door.

This, he thought, is what a saloon should be like.

Draped over drinkers' shoulders and across gamblers' laps were several attractive working girls who'd settled in with the winners at each table. Scanning the boisterous crowd, Clint could see no trace of Doc Holliday until the man's familiar hacking cough sounded above the racket.

Clint pushed through the people and made his way toward the faro tables in the back of the room. Sitting at the last table with his back to the corner was Doc, dressed in his usual black suit, white shirt, and string tie. The room was heating up from all the people in close quarters, and Doc's jacket was open to reveal a shoulder holster beneath his left arm in which he carried his nickel-plated Colt.

When Clint approached Doc's table, he noticed Doc was also wearing a holster on his right hip. Besides the ragged, bloody coughs, Doc's guns were his only constant companions.

Acknowledging Clint's arrival with a subtle nod, Doc finished the current hand and passed the cards over to the new dealer. He got to his feet without the use of his cane and even had a bit of spring in his step. As usual, Doc reeked of alcohol.

"Ah assume you have some business with me, so why don't we have a drink and get it out of the way," Doc said without slurring a single word.

He led the way to an empty spot at the end of the bar where they could have some degree of privacy. Before Clint could say a word, Doc was already on his second shot of whiskey.

"You haven't changed a bit," Clint said, "but I thought your game was poker, Doc."

"Ah don't mind bucking the tiger as long as Ah'm playing for the house. It was Wyatt got me interested in faro." Doc paused a moment, and Clint thought that the man was thinking of Wyatt in that moment fondly.

But that faded quickly.

"What's on your mind, Adams? Or did you stumble onto me by accident?"

"No accident, Doc. Actually, I was just next door at Bill Allen's. Business seems better over here. You must not be cheating the players as badly."

Grinning, Doc lost the tension he'd shown at the mention of Bill Allen's name and sank back into his usual relaxed manner—like a coiled snake relaxes before striking.

"Adams, you should know that faro is a game designed to make the house a profit. Even if Ah was to cheat, those skills wouldn't be needed."

Doc paused to remove a flask from his vest pocket and refill his glass before adding, "As for the patronage here, Ah must say the citizens of Leadville do have a bit of taste after all."

"What do you think of Bill Allen?"

"So that's what you wanted to know, is it?"

Clint nodded.

"Ah suppose he's already told you what he thinks about me."

Clint nodded again.

"Very well. Allen is a petty, loudmouthed, conniving idiot who's too busy strutting around his saloon to do the job his title demands."

"He mentioned something about you holding out on a gambling debt."

Doc stared for a moment, and Clint wondered if he was going to lose his temper.

"Ah'm sure he did. That man acts more like a spoiled child than a card player. What do you care, anyway, Adams? Are you takin' up bill collectin' now?"

"No, I just wanted to see how you answered the question."

Doc looked slightly puzzled and leaned back on his stool, holding his arms out to either side. "Well, did Ah pass?"

Relaxing for the first time since stepping foot into the bar next door, Clint allowed a smile to creep onto his face.

"Actually," he said, "I think I believe you more than I did the town's chief of police."

Staring into Doc's eyes, Clint could tell the pale man had nothing to hide. Normally, professional gamblers would sidestep any questions regarding their debts, or at least be offended by someone marching in and questioning them on the subject. Whatever Clint may have thought about Doc, he'd always known the man to be straightforward and direct, and he still had no reason to think otherwise.

"Is Allen crooked?" Clint asked.

Doc seemed to stare directly through the back of Clint's head. The intense blue eyes seemed strangely out of place in Doc's pasty, sunken face, as though they were too strong to be in such a frail-looking body.

"What do you think? You saw his operation."

"I think he's got pretty good dealers."

"And?"

"And I caught at least one of them cheating. Of course, that doesn't mean that Allen knows."

"Ah try to keep my distance from the man, and his operation. He wants nothin' more than to draw me into a fight over a five-dollar debt. Ah've never had much use for the law, but getting into a gunfight is precisely what Ah don't need right now . . . no matter what you've heard about me."

Clint started to say something, but Doc stopped him before any words escaped his lips.

"The truth of the mattah is that Ah don't care enough about Bill Allen to know if he's crooked or not. My primary concern of late has been keeping myself from putting a bullet through that flappin' mouth of his. Now, if you'll excuse me, Ah have some cards to deal."

Clint was surprised by two things: Doc extended his hand, and when they shook the man's grip was surprisingly firm. After shaking hands Doc headed back to the faro table.

Watching Doc wade through the crowd and seeing all the genuine affection heaped onto him by so many of the people there, Clint took a moment to reconsider the man. The Doc Holliday he thought he knew would have been chomping at the bit to put a bullet into Bill Allen.

For tonight, however, Doc Holliday seemed like a man doing his best to live under the cloud of a bad reputation. Surely, Clint could relate to that.

TWENTY-TWO

On a stretch of mountain road where the only man-made thing for miles in any direction was the road itself, the windy calm that usually surrounded the area was broken by the sound of two horses running at full gallop. It looked as if it was snowing, but that was only due to all the loose snow being kicked up and tossed about by the fierce wind.

The sun was falling below the horizon, giving the chill an extra bite as it whipped through the riders' coats. Hunching low in their saddles, both figures pulled their horses to a stop next to a huge fallen boulder on the side of the trail.

For a second they waited silently, neither wanting to remove the scarves from around their faces to talk. After a few minutes one of the men tugged at the thick material protecting his face and spit out a stray piece of wool.

"You sure we're supposed to meet him here, Charlie?" he asked.

The other man looked around for a few seconds then turned back to his partner and nodded.

"Shit, this cold is fierce! I swear this winter is gonna be somethin' else. Aw hell," he swore while pulling his coat closer around him. "It's always colder in the mountains, anyway."

The second man grumbled something from behind his scarf, but all that could be heard was a muffled groan.

"I can't hear what you're sayin'."

Impatiently, the other man pulled the dirty material away from his mouth and yelled, "I said stop your whinin' and keep an eye out. This ain't no picnic for me, either, you know."

"What if he doesn't show?"

"He'll show, Tom. With all he has invested in arranging for the law to let us do our business in private, he'll show all right."

As if on cue, a third rider appeared in the distance. This man, however, seemed immune to the cold, dressed in a simple riding coat and gloves. As opposed to the men waiting for him, the approaching rider's face was fully visible, but covered with a thick, brown beard that probably offered more warmth than any scarf.

The pair waiting for him next to the boulder could have been mistaken for two piles of coats and winter gear stacked on horseback if they hadn't started waving when he approached.

The third man returned the greeting, pulled up alongside the others and said, "Beautiful morning, don't ya think, fellas?"

Charlie blew warm air into the palms of his hands and rubbed them together vigorously.

"Cut the shit, Creek," he said. "Let's do this quick so I can get back in front of my fire."

"You first."

Swearing he could hear his spine creaking in the frozen air, Charlie swiveled in his saddle and removed a pair of heavy bags from where they'd hung over the back of his horse. Tom followed suit and produced a pair of similar bags from his own mount.

Turkey Creek Jack Johnson smiled from beneath his shaggy beard, and steam drifted up from between his teeth.

"Open 'em up," he said.

"Christ almighty, Creek," Tom bellowed, "we're freezin' our asses off and you don't trust us—"

Cutting him off in mid-sentence Creek swung his right arm from underneath his coat to reveal a fist clenched around a .45.

"Open up them bags, boys," he said. "Do it before I arrange for your bodies to get a lot colder."

Both Tom and Charlie knew they wouldn't be able to beat Creek to the punch, even if they hadn't had their hands full. More aggravated than frightened, they yanked open the drawstrings of their bags and held them wide open for Creek's inspection.

Johnson leaned forward and peered into the burlap sacks and nodded approvingly.

"Drop them to the ground."

They did as he ordered, and Creek swung down from his horse to fetch something from his saddlebags. Filling one of his ham-sized fists was a bundle of cash, tied together with a piece of twine. It was enough to make Tom forget about the snow frozen into his eyebrows. Leaning forward, he reached out for his prize, not minding the gun still held in Creek's other hand.

"Just one second," Johnson said as he cocked the hammer on the .45, bringing the weapon back to Tom's immediate attention. "Back off."

After Tom withdrew his hand, Creek stuffed the bundle of money inside his jacket and reached inside one of the bags. Grabbing from the bottom of the sack he pulled out a large piece of glittering rock that fit perfectly in his oversized palm.

Charlie and Tom exchanged nervous glances while Creek turned the gold nugget over in his hand. All the while Johnson's pistol held steady and perfectly still, aimed for a point directly between Tom's eyes. To the relief of both men, when Creek returned the nugget to the bag he was smiling.

"Everything looks all right to me," Creek said. Removing the money from his jacket he walked up to Tom's side, shifting his aim to cover the other man as he got closer.

Charlie continued warming his hands and began to fix the scarf back over his mouth. Before his face was covered he said, "Of course everything's all right. Hell, we'd never cheat you, Creek."

"Yeah," Tom said, while he snatched up the bundle of money and tucked it beneath his layers of shirts and coat. "The only thing that coulda spoiled this deal was the law, and we took care of that."

Creek backed away from the riders and gathered up all four burlap sacks. He flung them over both of his meaty shoulders with a rumbling sound but never buckled under the considerable weight.

"I know," Creek said. "Everything's handled, but a man can't be too careful."

Taking one step toward his horse Johnson looked over at Charlie and winked. "Or too rich, huh?"

Charlie laughed and bundled himself up for the ride back to the cabin he shared with Tom at a lower, warmer altitude. As Creek handled the bags of gold and loaded them onto his horse, the .45 was put away and all the tension between the men simmered down.

"Don't be a stranger, now," Tom said as his partner

began heading down the deserted trail. "It's been real good doin' business with ya."

The cold was starting to get to him again and Tom spurred his mount to catch up with Charlie, leaving Creek alone in the biting wind. Johnson loaded the bags over his horse's back and knew the extra weight would mean the trip back would be longer than he'd originally planned.

"Easy, now," Creek Johnson said to his horse. "It's not that far to Leadville and then you'll get a nice long rest."

Climbing into the saddle Creek turned up his collar and shook some of the snowflakes out of his grizzled beard. He'd always loved the cold, but city life was going to be a welcome change, for a while.

"We'll both get a nice, long rest. Hell, this ride'll all be worth it just to see the look on Doc's face when he sees what we brought him."

TWENTY-THREE

Even though crooked lawmen weren't his problem, Clint couldn't get his mind off the subject. When he'd talked with Chief Allen, Clint was sure the man wasn't telling the truth—he just didn't know if it had to do with gambling or the law.

Doc had made his feelings clear, but then again Doc never thought too highly of any servant of the law unless his last name was Earp. While he'd given up his own badge long ago, Clint still felt that he couldn't just sit back and let justice get trampled by anyone with enough money to do it.

"What's wrong, Clint?" Jeanette asked over a late dinner.

Clint poked at his steak and baked potato, trying not to look troubled. Obviously, he'd failed.

"I'm all right. Seeing Doc just brought back some old memories, that's all."

"Well, next time I won't let you wander around

town without a guide. I'm so sorry," Jeanette said.
"But I met with my suppliers today and now I'm all
yours for the rest of the trip." She reached under the
table to stroke his knee. "Did you miss me today?"

"Of course." All the same troubles still buzzed in
Clint's mind, making it hard for him to enjoy one of
the better steaks he'd tasted in quite some time.

Jeanette watched him and saw the distant look in
his eyes.

"Old memories, huh? Are we talking about Doc
Holliday, here?"

"Holliday, and the Earps."

"You mean Wyatt Earp, right?"

Clint nodded.

"I've known Wyatt for a long time. I feel badly because he's lost one brother, and the other's crippled."

"When is the last time you saw him?"

"I haven't seen him since the trouble in Tombstone. Ever since then, he's been . . . hard to keep
track of."

What he didn't tell Jeanette was the whole set of
new fears that arose when thinking about his old
friend. He knew Wyatt valued his family above everything else, and he also knew the deaths of the men
who shot down Virgil and Morg weren't coincidence.
Clint feared his friend had traded in all his values for
revenge. Only one man in town knew for sure and
Doc wasn't talking. His loyalty to Wyatt was com-
mendable, but it wasn't doing Clint any good.

Jeanette, however, was dazzled by the legend surrounding Wyatt and the battle at the O.K. Corral.

"Is Wyatt Earp everything they say he is?"

"I'm not sure how to answer that one," Clint said.
"I can tell you he's a hell of a man, and a great
friend."

She started to ask something, but Clint cut her off,
saying, "No, I wasn't at the O.K. Corral, but I was

damn close to being there when the shooting
started."

"What about Doc?" Jeanette asked, after Clint finished telling her about his time in Tombstone with
Wyatt. "I hear from some people that he's crazy.
They say he's mean to the core and a coldhearted
killer."

"Like I said before, I don't know Doc all that well,
but I can tell you one thing for sure. He's not crazy
and he's not just some mad dog killer."

"I know he's killed men," she said. "I've read it in
the papers."

Looking up from his now empty plate, Clint wiped
some gravy from his chin.

"Why all the sudden interest in killers and gunfights?"

Jeanette looked a little embarrassed and tried to
regain her normal composure.

"I admit that all the stories people tell when someone like Doc Holliday comes through town are exciting. Not all of us get to meet men like Wyatt Earp
or Wild Bill, you know. Most of us regular folks have
to settle for just hearing about them."

"Well, you may not believe this," Clint said. "But
sometimes I'd kill to have the normal life of a shop-
keeper or family man. I'll tell you one thing . . . every
one of those famous gunfighters you like hearing
about would probably tell you the same thing."

After paying for their dinner Clint followed Jeanette outside where the night's chill seemed to
chew its way through their clothes. Even though it
was getting late, there was plenty of activity going
on in the streets, and rowdy noise still poured out
from the area where most of the gaming halls and
saloons were concentrated.

As a breed, gamblers kept late hours. When a city
catered to them for any amount of time, it had to
shift its business schedules accordingly. Leadville

was no different. As they drew closer to Thirteenth Street, the energy level jumped up a few notches, spilling over to infect Clint and Jeanette.

"How about playing some cards?" she asked. "After all, this is where the money is."

Smiling down at his companion as they walked toward the part of town that would be hooting and hollering until sunrise, Clint could already feel the poker chips in his hands.

"I've always liked the way your mind works," he said.

TWENTY-FOUR

It was only a few hours before sunrise when Creek Johnson rode into Leadville. The ride was a bit longer, as he'd anticipated, due to the weight of the load he was carrying over his saddle. The sacks of nuggets thumped solidly against his horse's side, and the animal's breathing was becoming labored and ragged.

Pulling to a stop in front of Hyman's, Creek swung down, relieved his mount of the gold's weight, and lugged his cargo to the saloon's back door. Nobody on the street cared about where he was going, and the intense, burning look in his eyes discouraged even the slightest peek in his direction.

Johnson knocked three times on the bolted rear door and waited. "Aw, Jesus," he said when no answer came. Pounding fiercely on the door, he growled, "C'mon and open up! I'm not standin' out here all night."

Before Creek's fists did any permanent damage to the door, it was unlocked from the inside and slowly swung open to reveal the slender figure of Doc Holliday. Doc waved him inside and locked the door behind him.

"Subtle as always," Holliday said as he watched Creek set his burden on the floor. "Next time, why don't you shoot a hole through the front window? It would attract less attention."

"Christ almighty, Doc, at this hour there ain't a sober head in there. That's including you, I'll bet."

While Creek wasn't far from the truth, Holliday had been known to drink more than anyone had thought humanly possible and still ask for more. The former dentist's clothing reeked of tobacco smoke and stale liquor, but he stood bolt upright without the slightest hint of a waver in his voice.

"Is this all there was?" Holliday asked.

"Isn't it enough?"

Showing his first signs of fatigue, Creek allowed his huge, bearlike frame to fall into the only chair in the cramped back room. Meanwhile, Doc busied himself with examining the four bags and their contents. He removed one of the impressive nuggets and held it up to the light.

"I don't think I'll be happy until that stuff is out of my sight," Creek said. "That gold has become nothin' more to me than a weight around my neck. I damn near broke my back bringing it here."

If Doc heard Creek complaining, he gave no sign. Instead, he silently took a small leather case from a narrow shelf and emptied its contents onto a rickety table next to where Johnson sat rubbing his shoulders. The bag contained a knife, a piece of slate, and a glass vial full of acid. Using the knife, Doc shaved off a piece of the golden nugget in his hand and placed it onto the slate. Then he poured the acid onto the glittering sliver and waited.

As though nothing else were going on, Creek continued his bellyaching.

"We're damn lucky we got away with this one, Doc. The word's out on that stolen gold, and it took more than the usual price to keep the marshals off my back. More than once to and from the meet, I thought the law was breathing down my neck."

"There's nothin' to worry about, Creek. Ah'm sure our keepahs of the peace want their current state of wealth to continue," Holliday said while the acid bubbled and fizzled. "One word from us that they went back on our deal and the money stops coming."

Glancing over at the bulging sacks on the floor, Creek Johnson smiled and held a hand out to Doc. Without looking away from the smoking piece of slate, Holliday gave Creek his flask and Johnson took a healthy pull of whiskey.

"So tell me," Creek said. "How are you making out in town? Has your luck changed since Denver?"

"Not quite yet, but Ah still commute back and forth to Denver every week or so. That way, Ah've got two towns to work."

"There's no fire in your voice, Doc. Still flat broke, huh?"

"Ah prefer to think of mahself as between wins. You know how this game goes, Creek. The luck ebbs and flows."

"That's why I prefer to play games like this one," Creek said as he nudged one of the burlap sacks with his toe. "We've been pulling jobs like this for years together, and they have always paid more than poker ever did."

By now Doc was cleaning up the table and sweeping the slate clean of all the residue left from the melted nugget. With the effort, Holliday's breathing became louder and he straightened his stance to clear his throat. Before long, his coughing had in-

creased and he began wheezing into his white handkerchief.

"You all right, Doc?"

Doc held up his hand to keep Johnson back as the
coughing fit subsided and his breath leveled out.

"Our jobs always have been profitable, Creek, but
none have matched a good game of poker. That's one
of the few ways to reach out, sweep away another
man's money, put it in your pocket, and smile to his
face. Conning or stealing could nevah be that much
fun."

Standing, Creek put the test kit back onto the shelf
and allowed Doc to rest in the chair.

"Fun I can do without," Creek said. "What we've
got here is easy money, Doc . . . and lots of it."

"Well, there is one slight problem," Doc said as he
took back his flask and sniffed absently at the liquor.

"What's that, Doc?"

"What we got here is fool's gold . . . and lots of it."

TWENTY-FIVE

While the rest of Leadville slept, Hyman's was wide-awake and teeming with life. At this time of night only those truly dedicated to cards and drink were still in the smoke-filled room, and their energy reached out to all the like-minded people in the area. Suddenly, sleep and relaxation were last on Clint's mind.

Hyman's was infected with the gambling bug and Clint was far from immune.

"Have you ever seen Doc in his own element?" Clint asked.

"No. I've only seen him around Denver a few times and on the train. He seemed pretty sick."

Stepping into the bustling saloon, Clint took in the familiar surroundings and said, "Well, you've never seen Doc until you've seen him play poker. He drinks more than any man I've ever known and it only brings out the color in his cheeks. This is his place, so keep an eye out."

Instead of searching for Holliday, Jeanette surprised Clint by lacing her arm through his and holding on tightly.

"If I remember correctly," she said, "you know your way around a card table, yourself."

"I'll hold off on my bragging until I play a few hours. If the cards don't fall right, I can become just as broke as the next man."

"Maybe I'll bring you luck."

"Seems like I've done all right so far."

For the moment there wasn't an empty chair at any of the gaming tables. For close to an hour it seemed as though the roulette wheel never stopped spinning and the chips never stayed in front of the same man. Biding his time, Clint nursed a single beer while Jeanette started in on the hard liquor. His intention was to plant himself at a table for a full night's game, and he didn't want to hurt his chances by getting drunk.

Finally, just when the atmosphere was wearing off and Clint was starting to get impatient, a spot opened at one of the poker tables close to the faro game and Clint eased himself into the empty chair.

"The game's five-card draw, mister," the dealer said.

After buying his chips and accepting the first hand of the night, Clint settled into his seat and slipped on his game face. Behind him, Clint's good luck charm sat quietly to observe.

Although the other three men sitting around Clint's table didn't look like much, every one of them proved to be more than competent card players and each took turns giving Clint a run for his money. All were dressed in common street clothes that bordered on ragged.

On Clint's left, there was a man in his early forties sporting a thick black beard, marked with the occasional strands of gray. He kept conversation at the table going and was full of comments for his as well as everyone else's hand.

Sitting next to him was a younger man with shoulder-length hair who appeared to be in his mid-twenties. While he was more reserved than his neighbors, the cool blue eyes behind the rounded spectacles didn't miss much. His luck hadn't been holding up and his money was dwindling. Still, when he won, Clint noticed, he won big.

To Clint's right was a gentleman who looked as though he should be lecturing at the head of a classroom instead of spending his nights in a saloon playing poker. His face was covered with a thick gray beard that was neatly trimmed and seemed perfectly at home on his wide, friendly face. He didn't say much, but he had it where it counted, having taken the last hand with a full house.

Jeanette still seemed content to watch, even though it had been going on two and a half hours of solid playing. Before the next hand was dealt, she leaned forward and whispered into Clint's ear, "Where's Doc?"

Clint scanned the room and found the faro tables. After another few seconds he spotted Doc's thin, pale figure in the dealer's seat at the faro table. Doc was pulling in his winnings and smiling broadly, not showing any sign of discomfort or illness. A man in his element, indeed.

"There he is," Clint said, pointing to the faro table. "You keep an eye on him and you'll learn a thing or two. Just watching him play has taught me quite a bit about gambling."

Craning her neck for a better view of Doc, Jeanette strained to see through the thick, ever shuffling crowd. As she squirmed in her seat, the next round of cards was being dealt at Clint's table by the house dealer.

Clint was dealt a four card run but didn't get the fifth needed for a straight. The betting went on for several raises, and the kid with the glasses took the pot with a king-high flush. It had been a while since the kid had had a win, but the pile of chips in the middle of the table had proven to be worth the wait.

Jeanette once again leaned forward to speak while the cards were being shuffled.

"I'm going to stretch my legs for a little bit," she said.

"Tell Doc I said hello."

Jeanette got up and headed toward the faro tables just in time to see Doc pull a golden watch from his vest pocket. After checking the time, Doc excused himself from the table and made his way toward a room at the back of the saloon. He moved with easy grace through all the commotion but still carried his walking stick. He seemed to be feeling better, but not altogether well.

At Clint's table he took the next hand with two pair, sixes, and fives. Looking up after pulling in his money, he noticed Jeanette sitting near Doc's table, waiting for Doc to emerge from the back room.

Two more hands went by without any sign of Doc. The dark-haired man on Clint's left was about to drop out of the game by this time and the room seemed to be more alive than ever . . . especially at the faro table. Clint noticed this and found it odd for Doc to be missing out on the action.

Before he had time to ponder the situation any further something more pressing caught his attention. He didn't need to be concerning himself with Doc's affairs, after all. Especially when he'd just been dealt a full house.

Kings over threes.

TWENTY-SIX

"You lyin', dirty, cheatin' bastard!"

Those words came through the main room of Hyman's just as clearly as if they'd been spoken inside rather than from the street. All the faces turned toward the front door except for one. Sitting quietly at his table Doc went about his business as though nothing had happened.

Just under an hour ago Doc had reappeared from the back room, looking as though he was fighting to keep his temper under control. His eyes, normally sharp and focused, seemed fiery and bothered as they peered out from under a furrowed brow.

When he made his way back to his seat behind the faro table, the crowd had parted as though they could sense his darker mood. Where he usually had something to say when the dealing began, there was only silence.

Something was definitely bothering Doc, that

much was certain. The dark cloud remained over
Doc's head for the rest of the night, not to be replaced even by curiosity when the argument in the
street began.

The sounds of the quarreling men outside could
be clearly heard and the promise of gunplay hung
heavy in the air. The owner of the first voice was still
hollering as the brawl went from the street to the
boardwalk and back again. By the sound of it one of
the men was going to have to be carried back home.

Clint wasn't ready to abandon his spot just yet. For
the moment, it sounded like a fistfight and that was
nothing he was going to concern himself with.

The first shot cut through the air as the gamblers
were losing interest in the screaming match. Hot on
the trail of the initial shot a second bullet exploded
from outside and shattered Hyman's front window.
That caused everyone in the room to hit the floor
and crawl for cover—all except for Doc, and Clint.

As before, Doc remained perched in his chair,
looking around with a casual, slightly annoyed expression on his face. Gunshots never frightened Doc.
As far as anyone could tell, there was next to nothing
on earth that did.

Clint remained in his seat simply because he knew
the shot had accidently entered Hyman's. He was
merely alert for another, but not panicky, like all the
others in the room. He did, however, look around for
Jeanette and saw that she had taken cover underneath a table.

"Son of a bitch!" exclaimed one of the men outside. "You better hit me with your next shot, 'cause
you're a dead man if you don't."

That was enough to pry Clint from his seat. He felt
the need to intervene before another shot accidently
killed someone—or before the fools killed each
other.

Through his dark, gray-streaked beard, the man

who'd been sitting next to Clint all night smirked and shook his head.

"Oh, yeah," he said. "This happens all the time. That's why I left Dodge City. It was just getting too damn quiet."

Another shot crashed through the window and Clint left his seat and moved in a crouch toward the front of the room. He scanned the room for damage, but other than a few bottles behind the bar there didn't seem to be any. Doc was still in his chair behind the faro table, watching Clint with a bemused expression.

Clint stepped outside and located the two men who were fighting. One of them was standing in the doorway of Bill Allen's saloon. The other one, hollering threats and shooting his pistol wildly, stood in the street. He was so drunk his bullets were flying through the windows of Hyman's rather than Bill Allen's place.

"I didn't cheat ya, Henry," said the man in the doorway.

"Bullshit, Sam, you never played a straight game of cards in your life. Your only mistake was tryin' to pull yer two-bit tricks on me."

Staggering forward toward the boardwalk, Henry fumbled with his revolver, thumbing fresh rounds into it. Sam kept his position in front of Allen's with his right hand poised over his holster. Both men had obviously had more than their fair share of whiskey. It occurred to Clint that if Henry had fired at Sam he would have ended everything by now. They were probably more of a danger to everyone else than they were to each other.

At that point Clint saw Bill Allen step out of his place. He waited to see how the chief of police was going to handle the matter.

"What the hell's got into you two, shootin' up my town?" he bellowed.

"He cheated me out of everything I got," Henry said. "He done it before, but he's never gonna do it again."

"You know that's a damn lie," Sam said.

Allen situated himself in the street between the two men.

"If there's any cheating in my place, I'll take care of it. Now, I'm still the law here, and I'm telling you to put your gun down, Henry Fellows . . . and get your hand away from your gun, Sam Eliot."

Everything got quiet as Clint watched. He kept his eyes on Henry, the man whose gun was already drawn, figuring trouble would come from there.

"Get out of the way, Bill Allen," Henry said. "I'm gonna kill me a cheater."

"Get out of the way, Chief," Sam said, "I got a right to defend myself."

"Neither one of you is gonna do anything," Allen said. He walked directly to Henry Fellows and pushed him.

"Leave me alone, Allen! I got a free hand here. I made sure of that."

"Let's calm down before I forget we're all friends here, Henry," Allen said.

The comments of the two men, Henry Fellows and Bill Allen, instantly made Clint think about all the talk of law for sale. Was that what Henry was referring to?

"Allen, I said move," Henry shouted.

Instead of moving Allen put both of his hands on Henry's chest and shoved. The man was pushed back, off balance, and fell onto his butt. Allen then turned to face Sam Eliot.

Clint saw Henry raise his gun from the ground, obviously drunk enough to intend back-shooting Bill Allen. Without thinking Clint drew and fired. His shot struck Henry in the right shoulder, immediately deadening his arm, causing the gun to fall from his grasp.

Allen turned quickly, producing his own gun but immediately assessing that there was no need for it. He holstered it, walked over to where Henry was sitting, his left hand clutching his right shoulder, and picked the man's gun up from the street.

"Get up, Henry," he said, pulling the man to his feet. Henry cried out in pain, but Allen paid him no heed and pushed the man toward his saloon.

"You, too, Sam," Allen said. "Hand me your gun and get inside."

Sam obeyed, turning his gun over to Allen, who pushed both men ahead of him into the saloon.

Clint crossed over to Allen's and followed them inside.

Inside the saloon Henry was sitting in a chair, holding his shoulder, and Sam was standing against the bar. The bartender had a shotgun out and was holding it loosely in his hand.

"I suppose you think I owe you some thanks?" Allen demanded.

"Only if you'd like to thank me for saving your life," Clint said.

"I get paid to handle situations like this, Adams," Allen said. "I don't remember asking for your help."

"Well, if you'd stopped them before lead started flying into Hyman's—"

He stopped short when he saw the grin on Allen's face. He knew then that the chief had deliberately waited too long *because* the lead was flying into Hyman's, and not into his place.

"Your friend Henry was about to back-shoot you, Chief."

"Both of these men were drunk, Adams," the chief said. "That was plain to see. Henry couldn't have hit me if he tried."

"Next time," Clint said, "I'll just stand by and find out."

"You do that."

With the entire situation defused, the rowdy laughter and piano music started up again. Two uniformed policemen entered the saloon at that point and the two gamblers were taken away to jail.

"Go back to Hyman's, Adams," Allen said, moving closer so that only Clint could hear him.

"What did that man mean when he said he arranged to have a free hand, Chief?" Clint asked.

"Like I said," Allen replied, "he was drunk."

"Maybe he thought he had an ace up his sleeve."

Allen stepped close enough for Clint to feel his breath on his face.

"I know what you're hinting at, Adams," he said, "and I don't like it. I'm gonna forget it, though, because maybe you did save my ass out there in the street. Take my advice and go back to Hyman's before I change my mind."

As Clint stepped back into the chaos of Hyman's he saw that things were pretty much back to normal. Jeanette came walking up to him, smiling broadly. She didn't seem at all frightened by what had happened. If anything, it seemed to have the opposite effect on her. She seemed excited by it.

"Let's go back to the hotel," she whispered in his ear as she hugged him.

As Clint looked over her shoulder to where Doc Holliday was dealing again, he noticed the man smirking knowingly at him, probably because they both had something in common now.

They were both on Chief Bill Allen's bad side.

TWENTY-SEVEN

Creek Johnson stood at the far end of the bar, which was just about fifteen feet away from Doc Holliday's faro table. Having been roused from the back room after the streetside window was shattered by gunfire, Creek now stood where he could see what was going on.

Sometimes, Doc seemed none too concerned about his well-being. Ironically, when the bullets started flying, that casual attitude toward death was what kept him alive. Doc had nothing to lose and that was all the edge he needed in most situations.

Doc remained in his seat the entire time, casually shuffling a deck of cards. He didn't even flinch when another set of quick shots sounded. Doc only looked up when a man entered the bar and was greeted by a gorgeous brunette.

"Holy shit," Creek muttered when he saw who the man was.

Creek watched as the Gunsmith paused to look at Doc and then headed over to one of the poker tables where the game was already getting back on track. The incident outside had only lasted minutes, and that was more than enough time for the gamblers to resume their business.

After Clint Adams settled back into his game, Doc strode over to the bar and stood next to Creek.

"Ah'll have anothah," he said to the bartender.

In a few seconds Doc was handed a small drinking glass filled with whiskey. He polished off half of the healthy serving and cleared his throat before looking over at Creek Johnson.

"Are you through sulking?" he asked.

Ignoring the comment, Creek motioned toward Clint and asked, "Is that who I think it is?"

"That depends on who you think it is."

"C'mon, Doc, you know who I mean. Is that the Gunsmith playing poker over there?"

"Yes, it is, and Ah wouldn't call him that to his face if Ah were you."

"I'm curious, Doc," Creek said. "Bein' a friend of Wyatt Earp and all, whataya think of Clint Adams?"

"Other than Wyatt," Doc answered, "he is probably the one man Ah know of who impresses me . . . and Ah don't impress easily."

Creek looked surprised.

"Of course," Doc continued, "if you repeat that to anyone . . ."

"Oh, I won't, Doc," Creek said, "don't worry."

Creek ordered himself a beer and waited for it to arrive before continuing the conversation. His plans had already gone far enough off track and the last thing he needed was someone like the Gunsmith thrown into the works. He leaned closer to Doc.

"So, what happened out there?"

"Just a scuffle between a winner and loser from our next-door neighbor. A gentleman at mah table tells me Bill Allen stepped in and Mr. Adams, there, kept him from being back-shot. Seems one of the men involved didn't take too kindly to being denied the benefits he had apparently paid for."

"That Allen's a piece of shit," Creek said, "but I didn't know he was dirty. This could change things for us in this town."

Doc shook his head. "Ah don't think so. Things for us couldn't get much worse as far as Allen is concerned. First of all, Ah don't know for sure what kind of arrangement he had with the man. Second, ol' Bill has taken a dislike to me since you've been away."

"Why doesn't that surprise me?"

"He had a lucky streak going and won some money off of me. He says Ah owe him a few dollars more and Ah beg to differ. Ah'll pay mah debts, but Ah refuse to line the pockets of a lawman without getting anything in return. Anyway, he's been gunnin' for me, but he hasn't got the guts to face me like a man."

Waving to the bartender, Creek ordered another beer and laughed to himself. The one thing that never ceased to amaze him was just how much Doc Holliday could get away with. Gunfights, irritating lawmen, even the disease that wracked his body never seemed to put Doc down for very long. All things considered, Creek couldn't help but like the Georgian.

"All that aside," Creek said in an attempt to snap Doc's attention away from the gaming tables. "What do you propose we do with these four bags of worthless rocks sitting in the back?"

"Ah've been thinking about that very thing, Creek, and Ah've decided this doesn't have to be a complete loss. Not for us, anyway."

"We've been swindled, Doc, pure and simple. How do we come back from that? Hell, those boys that sold us them rocks could be anywhere by now!"

"True, we've been swindled. That only proves that it happens to the best of us." Doc didn't bother mentioning that *he* did not think he would have been fooled by the "fool's" gold if he had been the one examining it. Creek made a mistake, but there was no point in rubbing his face in it. What they had to do now was come back from it.

"Unlike those two that took us," he said, "we can't disappear after our mark discovers what they've got."

Rubbing his full, neatly trimmed mustache, Doc's eyes sparkled with the challenge in front of them.

"The job will require a little more finesse," he said, "but Ah still think we can pull it off. Let's take some time to think the matter through and we'll come up with something."

"What the hell," Creek said, slapping the wooden planks making up the bar in front of him. "Let's do it."

TWENTY-EIGHT

For the next few days Clint took a more active
interest in finding out what made Bill Allen tick. Although he didn't know how many people were in
Leadville, by the time he got finished asking questions around town the word was out on who he was
and they all seemed to have the same speech pre-
pared for him.

"He's a stand-up man," some would say.

"Bill don't take nothin' from nobody," others
would say.

While none of what folks said was really bad, it
wasn't necessarily good, either. All Clint could
gather from his efforts was that Chief Allen was a
hard-ass who had no love for Doc Holliday. That second part seemed to be common knowledge in the
gambling section of town.

After the three days he spent checking into Allen
and the gambling at Hyman's and Allen's saloons,

Clint wasn't much farther along than when he had started. Since it wasn't his job to catch crooked lawmen, Clint decided to conduct his business as it came his way and focus on his poker playing. That part, at least, was going well, as he seemed to be on a winning streak.

Jeanette didn't seem to be sharing Clint's growing affection for Leadville. As the sun started fading from the view of their suite at the Four Star Hotel, she came up behind him and snaked her arms around his chest, laying her head against his back.

"Clint, don't you think it's about time we headed back to Denver?"

"Actually, I was planning on staying here at least another few days." Seeing the unhappy look in her eyes as he swiveled around to face her, Clint held her at arm's length. "No more than a week, though. After that everything here should be wrapped up and we can have one more night just to ourselves."

"Can't you drag yourself away from that damned saloon to be with me for just one night?"

Until this moment Clint had completely forgotten about this side of Jeanette. While she was one of the sweetest women he'd known, she was spoiled and used to having her own way. Last time, he'd been forced to leave because she'd been getting too attached to him and way too possessive.

"It's not that," Clint said. "I've been checking around lately, asking about Bill Allen, and there really seems to be some bad blood between him and Doc. Remember how we were talking about the crooked lawmen in this area?"

"Yes."

"I think men show their true colors when they're angry, and Doc seems to be the one setting off Allen's temper. If I can be here when Allen tips his hand, I'll know for sure if he's honest or not. Besides, if he is crooked, he might be looking for any reason to string Doc from a noose."

"I thought you didn't care much for Doc."

"He's not a good friend, but he's no enemy. If anything, I owe it to Wyatt to keep Doc from being railroaded."

Jeanette pulled away from Clint, turning her back to him. When she turned back around, her arms were folded across her chest and her face was cold with anger.

"I have to get back to Denver sooner than that and I'm getting sick of not seeing you. I'll be on tomorrow's train and if you're not with me, I hope you'll visit before taking off and leaving the area."

Clint put his hands on her shoulders and pulled her to him.

"You're right," he said, holding her even though she was stiff in his arms, "you have to get back to your business. I'll be finished here before you know it, and I will see you again before I leave Colorado."

She wilted in his arms and pressed herself against him. She looked up at him and they kissed deeply.

"I forgot about the problems we had last time," she said. "We both have strong wills."

"Yes, we do."

"All right . . ." she said, letting her voice trail off.

She kissed him again, squirming against him, then started to kiss her way down his body until she was kneeling in front of him.

"You'd better see me before you leave the state," she murmured, "but meanwhile, I'll give you a little something to remember me by."

She stroked his erect cock until it grew harder, then caressed it with the tip of her tongue. Looking up at him she said, "A little good-bye kiss before we part company."

Before he could say anything she took him fully into her mouth, pumping her head vigorously back and forth. If there was any doubt that he would stop in Denver to see her again, it was gone.

She sucked him for a few more minutes, then stopped, took him by the cock, and drew him to the bed. There, Clint forgot all about Doc Holliday and Bill Allen . . . for a while.

TWENTY-NINE

The train to Denver had pulled out of the station hours ago, but the Gold Strike Saloon was just beginning to show signs of life. Kit Farrell was starting the day picking up the bits of glass and cigar butts left over from the previous night.

Most gambling houses never closed, but Farrell also had a hotel to run and his guests needed their peace and quiet. He didn't even open his doors until the afternoon and that was precisely why Doc stayed there, even while he did his faro dealing and gambling at Hyman's. At twenty minutes to noon the Gold Strike was dead quiet, with only the occasional sound filtering into the main room.

Like the cry of a sick rooster, Doc's hacking cough told those staying at Farrell's that it was time to get up. Anyone sleeping later than Doc was usually ill or still drunk from the night before.

"Mornin', Kit," Doc said as he staggered down the

stairs, pulling his suspenders up over his thin shoulders. He was without his usual black coat, which placed his shoulder holster in plain sight. The nickel-plated .45 caught the rays of the sunlight coming in the window.

Farrell already had a cup of coffee waiting on the bar for Doc.

"More like afternoon, Doc. How are you feelin' today?"

Dabbing at a little drop of blood in the corner of his mouth, Doc laughed and picked up the cup of coffee.

"Oh, just perfect. Ah'm just happy to wake up to anothah day of sunshine and roses."

As he sipped the steaming brew, Doc squinted painfully when he stepped into a beam of light that cut right through the dust upset by his footsteps.

"Now, if that damn sun wasn't so bright Ah'd be even happier."

"I know how you feel," Farrell said, although he didn't.

Doc took the coffee back to his room and reappeared soon after fully dressed in his coat and hat and carrying his walking stick.

"Ah think Ah'll take a walk this mornin'," Doc said as he set the empty cup back on the bar. "Does Sally still serve breakfast this time of day?"

"I'm sure she'll find you something, Doc," Farrell said. "She's got a soft spot for you."

"If you started serving food here you'd save me a trip," Doc said.

"If I started servin' food they'd hang me for killin' my customers," Farrell said. "Remember the last time I tried to cook?"

Pausing in front of the door, Doc thought for a moment before nodding solemnly.

"Good point. Ah'm the only one who survived that meal and look at the fine specimen Ah've become. But," he added as he went out the door, "did it ever occur to you to hire somebody?"

THIRTY

Walking out onto the battered boardwalk, Doc took in a ragged breath and started toward one of his favorite restaurants for a thick steak and some fresh eggs, providing Sally was still serving it. This was the first day since his arrival that he had awakened with an appetite.

Along the way a younger man fell into step with Doc. He was fresh-faced and in his early twenties. He was wearing a simple brown suit and matching derby. His hair was brown and in need of cutting, hanging in front of eyes that were alert and searching. Even the way he walked betrayed his eagerness. The younger man was E. D. Cowen, a reporter for *The Leadville Democrat*, who had helped Doc out of a particularly sticky situation that had followed him from his days in Tombstone.

"You headin' to Sally's?" Cowen asked.

"Sure enough. Care to join me for a steak?"

The younger man nodded, and his chest swelled with pride at the invitation.

"We should make it before Sally gives up on breakfast. This town's full of late risers like yourself, Doc. I haven't seen you around the past few weeks. Where've you been hidin'?"

"Ah was back in Denver for a spell, but Ah came back to town a few days ago. The hospitality here calls me back whenever Ah stay away too long."

Cowen laughed but then the smile dropped from his face when he saw the figure that was coming from the opposite direction.

"Don't look now," he said, "but here comes your own personal welcome wagon."

Doc had already seen Bill Allen coming, but kept quiet. Now, as the bulky man approached, Doc's blue eyes narrowed into burning, intense slits. Chief Allen walked up to Doc and Cowen, stopping directly in front of them to block their path.

"Good day, suh," Doc greeted. "We were just headed off to fill our stomachs at Sally's. Perhaps you'd care to join me later for a game of cards? Oh, but Ah forget, you're not much of a gambler, are you?"

Cowen knew all about the chip Allen was carrying around on his shoulder for Doc and couldn't hold back a smile at Doc's comment. The reporter had liked Doc instantly after meeting him for the first time two years ago and that was largely due to Doc's dry sense of humor. Sometimes, as now, the Georgian thrived on pissing people off.

"Up yer ass, Holliday," Allen grunted. "You can go eat shit for breakfast for all I care. You got my money or not?"

"Ah've got enough for a rare piece of steak and some eggs, but that's all." Taking one step more Doc stood eye to eye with Allen and, giving credit to the chief of police, he never backed off. Cowen took in the whole scene with a reporter's keen eye.

"Why don't you sell that badge of yours for five dollars?" Doc suggested. "That's about all it's worth."

The police chief's hand moved toward the gun on his hip, but he didn't draw. Instead, he shifted his weight and took a few steps back to put some distance between Doc and himself. For a second, Cowen thought the lead was going to fly, and he started to quietly back away from the two men.

Bill Allen looked ready to explode with anger as his hand hovered over the butt of his pistol. Standing perfectly still, Doc simply glared back with his left hand on his cane and his right hanging loosely at his side.

In Doc's eyes there was no fear. He was ready for a point-blank fight, but he wasn't the least bit nervous.

As though sensing Doc's almost suicidal readiness to fight, Bill Allen suddenly relaxed his posture and started to walk away.

"You'd best come up with the money soon, Doc," he said. "Pay your debts like a man."

With that he turned his back on Doc and walked across the street. Cowen moved back to Doc's side and said nothing as they watched Allen walk away.

"Ready for that steak?" Doc asked him.

Shaken, Cowen nodded. He was amazed at Doc's coolness in the face of Allen's aggressive nature, and even more amazed that the chief of police had backed off. He was sure the man had been ready to go for his gun.

He wondered which Doc enjoyed more. Forcing a man to back down simply with a look? Or staring into the face of danger . . . or maybe even death?

Before Cowen could decide, Doc was off and he had to trot to keep up.

When they reached the restaurant Doc put his

hand on Cowen's arm to stop him before they entered.

"Ah wish you'd do me a favor."

"What's that, Doc?"

"Bill Allen is after me, and sooner or later he'll force the issue. Ah want you to be around to watch me wing him when the ball comes off."

Opening Sally's door, Doc wore an expression that was part disgust and part annoyance.

"He isn't worth killing," he added.

THIRTY-ONE

After a leisurely breakfast Clint headed over to Bill Allen's place. He figured he'd better clear the air between himself and the local law after what had happened. Also, it would be easier to keep an eye on the man when he could approach him without making a scene.

Bill sat at one of the tables along the far wall, going over his books, not even looking up as Clint walked through the door. The bartender snapped to attention and headed toward Clint's end of the long, spotless bar.

"What can I get for ya?"

Clint was looking in Bill Allen's direction when he said, "Coffee, black."

When he got his drink Clint walked across the empty room and pulled up a chair at Allen's table, sitting down across from the chief of police.

Without looking up from his ledger Allen muttered, "What do you want, Adams?"

"I just wanted to make sure there were no hard feelings between us after the other night in the street. I'm sorry if I stepped on your toes, but it looked to me like—"

"You did step on my toes, Adams," Allen interrupted, finally looking up from his paperwork. "You also shot a man right in front of me."

"I was trying to help you."

"That's why I have deputies. You're not one of them."

Shaking his head, Clint broke the tension that was starting to form and held his hands in front of him, palms facing out.

"I don't want to fight with you, Allen. I just wanted to clear the air and make sure I was on good terms with the law."

"I've heard all about you, Adams, and I appreciate your help, but I don't want to encourage any gunplay in my town. Furthermore, if you want to stay on the good side of the law, you'd best keep away from that sickly friend of yours."

Clint nodded and took a sip of coffee. He could tell from the first time he'd met Bill Allen that Doc had been getting to him. It was no real surprise. Doc got to a lot of people.

"Besides the money he might owe you, it looks to me like Doc is minding his own business."

"He's been biding his time . . . waiting."

"Waiting for what?"

Shoving his ledger aside, Allen leaned forward and stabbed a meaty finger in the direction of Hyman's.

"He's been waiting for his friend to arrive. Him and Creek Johnson have something going on and it ain't simple business. Now that Creek's in town, I aim to put a stop to whatever it is."

"What if it's legal?"

Allen laughed shortly, almost a bark.

"Not likely."

Clint had seen Turkey Creek Johnson once or twice several years ago. The burly bear of a man had been known to take an illegal job or two for fast money, but Clint had never heard him described as an outlaw of any kind. As far as him being in Leadville, Clint decided to take Allen's word for it.

"What does Creek Johnson have planned?" he asked.

"This is police business, Adams, and I don't take to discussing it with civilians over coffee. Now, if you want to play poker or have a drink, you're welcome to stay. If you want to keep hounding me for information about official business, you can leave. If you want to stay out of trouble and in one piece . . . I suggest you stay away from that good-for-nothing runt Holliday."

Bill Allen, Clint decided, was a lost cause. The man had a chip on his shoulder the size of his bulky ledger when it came to Doc Holliday. Whether or not he was crooked Clint still couldn't say. While he was certainly unlikable, Allen's manner did not necessarily mean he was dishonest.

Clint finished his coffee, stood up, and walked out. He may not have been a lawman, but you didn't need a badge to know that when Bill Allen and Doc Holliday finally collided, sparks were going to fly.

THIRTY-TWO

Walking out of Allen's saloon Clint couldn't help but notice a large, barrel-chested man heading straight for him. When he drew closer Clint saw that the other fellow was about an inch or so taller than he was but had to have about fifty extra pounds of bulk.

He wore battered jeans and a ragged fringed jacket over a worn-out flannel shirt. Although the man's beard all but covered his face, a look of surprise still made its way through the mask of grizzled hair.

Clint hadn't seen the man more than a handful of times before, but he instantly recognized him. After all, Turkey Creek Johnson was a hard man to forget.

The surprise on Creek's face quickly turned into a smile as he made his way to Clint's side.

"Clint Adams, how the hell are ya?" Creek asked, sounding as though they were long lost friends.

Although Clint felt uncomfortable, Creek's warmth

was infectious and the two men shook hands.

"You're Jack Johnson, aren't you?"

"Aw, call me Creek."

Clint could almost feel Allen's stare through the saloon's front window. After the talk they'd just had he decided to try to move this conversation to a different place.

"I was just taking a stroll around town, Creek," he said. "Care to join me?"

Falling into step beside Clint, Johnson walked for half a block with him without saying a word. He seemed to be honestly taking in the sights and surveying the area, completely oblivious to the chilly breeze that whipped through town.

"What brings you here, Creek?" Clint asked, as innocently as he could.

"I'm here for the same reason everyone else is, I guess," Creek said. "The money."

Clint nodded and smirked at that statement. He'd always fancied himself a gambler, but being back in a money town always made him feel like an amateur. He had the skill at cards and knew how to win, but he didn't have the fanatical desire of men like Doc Holliday, and Luke Short, who could smell a winning streak the way a bloodhound smells wild game.

"I'm not one of these big-time card sharps, though," Creek added. "I'm also here to see Doc. Poker's more his game. We go back a long ways, Doc and me. I don't know if you knew that."

"I've heard."

"What about you?" Creek asked. "Are you here for the cards?"

"Partly," Clint said with a shrug. "I came here with a lady friend and she had to head back to Denver. I thought I'd stay and see how my luck held out."

"You ask me, yer better off without some woman lookin' over yer shoulder," Creek said, slapping Clint on the back. "For a while Doc thought his Kate was a good luck charm, and she's almost been the death of him more times than I can count."

"Some women are better than others, I guess," Clint said.

"Ain't that the truth," Creek said, shaking his head. "I say stick with whores. You get what you need, pay fer it, and move on."

Again, Clint just shrugged. He made it a rule never to pay for sex. He'd never had to.

At the end of the block, next to a barbershop and across from the town undertaker, Creek stopped and turned to face Clint.

"Why don't you stop by Hyman's tonight and I'll buy ya a drink. Or do you prefer Bill Allen's?"

Clint had the feeling he was being tested. Creek Johnson had asked the question in apparent innocence, but he was watching Clint much too carefully, waiting for the answer.

"No, I prefer Hyman's," Clint said. "I was just at Allen's straightening out a misunderstanding."

"He seems to have those with a lot of people," Creek said.

"Sure seems that way."

"The way you came out of there, knowing what I know about you, I thought you'd signed on with ol' Bill."

Obviously, what Creek Johnson knew about Clint was all wrong.

"Bill Allen can handle his town without me."

"Did ya settle yer disagreement?"

Clint shook his head.

"Never did."

"Tell ya what," Creek said. "You come to Hyman's tonight and I'll buy ya that drink. Me, you, and Doc can sit around and swap some lies."

"Sounds good to me."

"Great! I'll keep a table cleared fer us."

Thinking his curiosity would soon be the death of him, Clint still wanted to spend some time with Doc and Creek to try to find out what the pair really were up to, if anything.

At the very least, they'd be better company than Bill Allen.

THIRTY-THREE

Sally's was one of Leadville's largest restaurants. No matter what time of day it was, the place seemed crowded. The owner, Sally Hackett, was in her early forties but had the energy of a saloon girl half her age. Every person that came through her door was greeted with a booming hello and a strong handshake. She was not a small woman by any means, but her personality would have seemed out of place coming from a petite body.

When Creek Johnson entered the place, he had to stop and scan the busy dining room for a minute or so before he found who he was looking for.

"Hello, there, big man!" Sally bellowed as she approached Creek. "Yer new here, ain't ya, honey? What can I get for you?"

Looking over Creek's burly frame and rugged features, she placed her hands on her hips, looking as

though she were about to lick her lips in anticipation.
"For you, the sky's the limit."

Finally, Creek spotted Doc's table toward the back
of the room.

"I'm meeting someone here and I just found him."

Sally followed Creek's gaze and said, "You're with
Doc? Why didn't ya say so? Go on over, if he's ex-
pectin' ya."

Creek walked over and noticed that there was already someone sitting next to Doc. Both men were
just starting in on thick cuts of steak and fresh eggs
when Creek sat down next to E. D. Cowen.

Looking up from his meal, Doc hurriedly chewed
on a bite of steak before greeting Johnson with a lazy
wave of his fork hand.

"You're late, Creek. We started without you. E. D.
Cowen," Doc said, motioning to the slender young
reporter next to him, "meet Jack Johnson."

"Call me Creek."

Wiping his hands on a napkin before extending a
handshake to Creek, Cowen smiled.

"I'm a reporter for *The Democrat*, Creek. I seem
to have heard of you—"

"Yeah," Creek interrupted. "You might have heard
the stories, but don't believe a word Doc says. He's
always been jealous of me 'cause I'm prettier than
he is."

The delicious aroma in the room convinced Creek
to order the steak breakfast, and the rest of the meal
passed with relaxed conversation. Mostly, however,
Cowen did the talking while Doc and Creek sat back
and listened to the reporter's retelling of the current
events and gossip. Finally, Cowen said it was time
for him to leave and excused himself from the table.

"Seems like a nice enough young fella," Creek
said, as Cowen paid his respects to Sally and left.

"He's good in small doses, but Ah'm most grateful

for your timely rescue," Doc said. "What have you
been up to?"

"I met up with Clint Adams on the way over here
and had a little talk with the man. Seems he'd been
to see Bill Allen and it looks like he's not workin'
with the law, after all."

"Ah told you not to worry about that. Ah may not
know Adams real well, but he's got more sense than
to work alongside a piece of scum like Allen. Did
you find anything else out?"

Creek started to answer but held his tongue when
the waitress came to clear the table and refill their
coffee cups.

"Not really," he said when she finished. "I did in-
vite him to Hyman's for a drink tonight, though."

"Ah'll be busy, but you can entertain him."

Pausing to take a healthy sip of coffee, Doc leaned
back in his chair, feeling better than he had in some
time.

"Doc, when do we unload those rocks?"

"We meet with a man from Chicago the day aftah
next. With a little practice beforehand it should be
no problem convincing him of the quality of the merchandise."

Creek raised his mug and smiled broadly from beneath his shaggy beard.

"Well, here's to four bags of useless rocks," he
said.

Holding his own mug, Doc finished the toast.

"May they prove to be otherwise."

THIRTY-FOUR

When Clint walked into Hyman's later that evening he was surprised to find more than one empty table and some space to stand at the bar. Even a money town has to rest sometimes, he thought.

After a quick scan of the room Clint spotted Doc and Creek sitting at a poker table toward the back. He made straight for it and sat down next to Creek and across from Doc.

Without so much as a word of acknowledgment, Doc tossed in his ante and dealt each man seven cards, including Clint. This was obviously Doc's game, as there was no house dealer, and the deal was passing from man to man.

After the deal made a full circuit around the table Doc broke the uneasy silence, pushing away from the stack of chips in front of him and getting to his feet.

"Who wants a drink?"

Nobody replied, and Clint followed. He assumed that Doc made the offer but no one took him up on it.

Clint had taken two of the five hands, and that put him ahead. In one of the hands it came down to him and Doc, and Doc had not called his final bet. The gambler knew that Clint wasn't bluffing, even though the game had been seven-card stud and most of Clint's full house had been hidden.

When Clint saw that Doc meant to have his drink at the bar, he excused himself and went to stand next to him.

"Beer," he said to the bartender.

"Ah thought you didn't drink when you played cards?" Doc asked.

"I'm not playing cards right now," Clint said. "Don't worry. I'll finish it here and not take it back to the table."

Doc finished his whiskey and had another. He downed the whiskey as if it were his life's blood, and none of the burn showed on his sunken face.

"Not dealing faro tonight, Doc?" Clint asked.

"Takin' the night off," Doc said, "to play a little poker."

Clint wondered if, when Creek Johnson invited him, the man knew that Doc would be playing poker tonight.

"Ah understand you spent some time with Bill Allen today," Doc commented. "He doesn't like gunmen in his town. Perhaps you should reconsider staying around here."

"That's what I wanted to talk to you about, Doc," Clint said. "Is there someplace private we can talk?"

Doc considered that for a moment, sizing Clint up with intense blue eyes that suddenly seemed to turn icy cold. Not sure how far to trust Clint, Doc remained silent for only a few seconds, weighing the pros and cons in an instant.

"Sure," he said finally, pointing to a door in the back wall. "Have a seat in there and Ah'll join you in a minute."

Clint made his way past the bar and into what appeared to be a storage room. Scanning the shelves and dirty floorboards, he thought the single table and chair looked more than a little out of place in the closet-sized room. It wasn't long ago that he had been in a similar room with Jeanette, behind her store in Denver.

At first he hadn't thought it necessary to close the door while waiting for Doc. When his eyes stumbled upon the four burlap sacks lying in the corner, he thought otherwise. One of the sacks sagged open to reveal a tough, glittering stone and Clint walked over to investigate, quietly shutting the door first.

Not knowing how much time he had, Clint knelt over the open bag and removed one of the smaller rocks. Turning it over in his hand, he stood to examine it under the dim light provided by the single lantern hanging from the ceiling.

The nugget sparkled with a glow that was both dull and brilliant, if that was possible. Clint nudged the sacks with a toe and knew that all of them were probably stuffed with a similar load.

Before he could calculate what such a treasure might be worth, Clint could hear footsteps approaching and the door began to swing inward. He hurriedly stuck the nugget into his pocket and stepped away from the corner just before Doc Holliday strode through the door with a flask of whiskey in his hand.

"Our chips are safe, but Ah can feel the cards growing cold. Let's make this quick and continue with our game, shall we?"

"I figured the folks here would know better than to fool with the chips you left on the table, Doc. Still, I thought it best to talk to you alone. With the kind of enemies you tend to make, I have no idea who could be listening, or what they'd think of what I had to say."

"Go ahead, Adams. You have mah undivided attention," Doc said as he settled himself into the rickety chair and set his flask on the small wooden table.

"You already know I've been talking with Bill Allen. From what he's been telling me, you two are on your way to drawing blood, and I sure would hate to see that happen."

"You wouldn't have to see anything if you kept to your own affairs."

"This is true," Clint said, "but whether either of us likes it or not I'm involved simply because I can't stand by and watch you gun down a lawman."

"And here Ah thought you were worried for my safety," Doc said with a theatrical sadness in his voice.

"I know you well enough to know that a man like Bill Allen has no chance at outdrawing you, Doc."

"Ah am not a killer."

Suddenly, Clint was growing tired of the conversation. As he headed for the door he said, "I just thought I'd let you know that Allen is chomping at the bit to draw down on you, Doc. Of all the things you need right now, killing a lawman is not one of them. You'd die in jail."

"We all have to die sometime," Doc said, "and somewhere."

"I'm not going to stand by and let you gun down the chief of police over a penny-ante gambling debt, Doc."

"Why?"

"What?"

"Why are you concerned?"

"We have a friend in common, Doc," Clint said. "I'd never be able to face Wyatt if I let you do something this stupid."

"Your point is well taken," Doc said. "Let me assure you that, as much as Ah'd like to send Bill Allen to his Maker, Ah do realize how messy that could be. Also . . . Ah appreciate your concern. There's plenty of men out there waiting for me to make a mistake just so they can be the ones to hang me the next mornin'. Now, do you want to play some more cards, or are you tired of losin' your money?"

"I'm about due for my winning streak," Clint said. Feeling the weight of the small nugget in his pocket he added, "I got what I came for, anyway."

THIRTY-FIVE

After an all-night poker session, Clint finally decided to pack it in once it was made clear to him that Doc Holliday had more than earned his reputation as one of the country's best poker players—on this night, anyway. Clint wondered how Doc would fair in a game with Luke Short and Bat Masterson.

Back in his room at the Four Star, Clint decided to change rooms in the morning. With Jeanette gone he no longer needed a suite. A regular room would do him just fine. In fact, maybe he'd even change hotels. The Four Star was a bit fancy.

Clint hung his gun belt on the bedpost, sat on the edge of his bed, removed his boots, and took the nugget from his pocket. Turning it over in his hand he noticed that a sliver of the rock had been sliced away, leaving a rough cross section exposed to the light.

Clint wasn't sure that those sacks had anything to

do with Doc and Creek. In fact, Doc had never even looked at them while they were talking. Something didn't seem right about them, though. Those bags, together with Bill Allen's suspicion that some big deal was going down, seemed like too much of a coincidence. Also, Clint wondered, what were four sacks of gold nuggets doing on the floor of some storage room and not in a bank vault or a safe somewhere?

Letting his fingers trail over the surface of the rock, Clint suddenly realized what had been troubling him about the nugget.

He'd seen a lot of gold in his time. After a while, a man gets to know what it looks like, how it feels, even how it smells and tastes. While Clint was certainly no expert, he knew gold when he saw it, and the rock in his hand was not it.

Normally, fool's gold was easily spotted by an experienced eye, but the sample Clint was holding looked so close to the real thing it had made a temporary fool out of him.

Surely, Clint thought, if those bags belonged to Doc, he knew what he had. The real question was . . . what was he going to do with them?

After Clint left Hyman's, Doc had moved away from the game to a table where he sat alone. Had Clint seen the sacks in the back room? Had he looked in them? And if he did, would he know what was in them?

And if he did, what would he do about it?

Doc appreciated the concern Clint Adams apparently had for him, even if it was only out of friendship for Wyatt Earp. He just hoped Clint Adams wouldn't get in his way, because how could he ever explain to Wyatt that he'd had to kill his friend, the Gunsmith?

THIRTY-SIX

"Where's Doc?" Clint asked.

By now it had become habit for him to wake up, grab a quick breakfast, and head down to Hyman's. This morning, though, he had also taken the time to change hotels, checking out of the Four Star and into the Golden Nugget—which he considered ironic, since he still had the nugget of fool's gold in his pocket.

The bartender shrugged and said, "I ain't seen him yet, but Creek's been by. He came around to fetch his gear and some other things from the back and then headed out. Ain't seen him since, neither."

Clint didn't even have to look in the back room to know what would be missing.

"When was this?"

" 'Bout twenty minutes ago?"

"I'll see if I can find him."

With that Clint went outside and quickly made his

way to the livery. He didn't know if Doc was with Creek, but maybe he could catch up and find out, or at least see which way Creek was headed, with or without Doc. As he approached the large, shabby-looking livery stable he noticed another figure entering the building.

The other man was bulky, but not bulky enough to be Creek Johnson. Although the swagger and scowl gave him away from fifty yards, the ornate badge on his chest let the world now that Bill Allen was coming through.

Clint waited until Allen was inside the stable before drawing closer to the building. It didn't take long for the men inside to notice each other, and soon their voices were raised in a fiery argument. Standing just outside the side door Allen had used, Clint listened to what was happening inside.

"Where the hell's my money?" Allen boomed.

Doc's voice began to answer but was cut off by a rough series of coughs that sounded painful, causing even Clint to flinch.

"Yer actin' like some spoiled little kid," Creek Johnson's voice said. "You'll get yer five stinkin' dollars when we get back."

"This ain't about the money. This is about treatin' me with respect."

"You're a real important man, Bill," Doc's voice drawled. "Ah'll pay you like Ah would anyone else."

Allen's temper cooled a few degrees, but his voice was still trembling with suppressed violence.

"If it was anyone else, Doc, I'd have what you owe me already."

There was a tense silence during which Clint wished he could see what was going on. He was about to risk a peek inside when Doc's voice broke the silence, although Clint could barely make it out.

"Anyone else wouldn't have given me this much trouble, Bill," Doc said. "Ah suggest you calm yourself down before you take this disagreement of ours further than you can handle."

"Let's see how you handle this, Doc," Allen grunted. "You pay me my money tomorrow or you'll be going to your own funeral."

"Don't try it, Bill," Doc said. "Unless you've come with both hands full of guns."

Another tense silence followed, and soon heavy footsteps began pounding toward the door. Clint barely got himself away from the livery before Chief Allen came thundering through the door, charging across the street like a man possessed.

The chief of police never even bothered to look anywhere but straight ahead and failed to notice Clint standing no more than ten feet away from him. As Allen turned a corner, Clint heard the sounds of the larger doors on the other side of the stable being opened and a pair of horses trotted out onto the street.

Glancing around the building, Clint saw Doc and Creek riding north, heading for the trail out of town. Before they broke into a gallop, Clint managed to get one clear glance to verify what he'd only suspected before.

Sure enough, on the backs of both animals, there were two burlap sacks thumping heavily against the horses' flanks. In his mind's eye, Clint could almost see the fool's gold in the sunlight.

Waiting until Doc and Creek were well out of sight, Clint entered the livery and found Duke. He hadn't seen much of the black gelding since he'd taken him off the livestock car of the train from Denver.

Duke grew anxious the minute he saw Clint.

"Easy, boy," Clint said, saddling the huge gelding. "Sorry I haven't been around, but we're going to go for a quick ride, now."

The horse's sinewy muscles flexed beneath the taut skin, and when Clint mounted and urged him forward, Duke charged outside like a sleek, black bullet that couldn't wait to leave the barrel of a gun.

It didn't take much for Clint to pick up the trail left by Doc and Creek. Apparently, the men were headed toward a nearby lake that was less than two hours' ride away. Halfway there, Clint had to fight to keep Duke from using all of his pent-up energy to race past the men they were following. He didn't even try, however, to keep the smile from his own face.

Sometimes, he swore that Duke could even outrun the wind.

THIRTY-SEVEN

The weathered old cabin sat perched on the edge of a dirty lake. Its walls looked as though termites were the only things keeping the pieces of wood together. Doc and Creek came to a stop in front of the battered dwelling and tied their horses next to a young brown colt. Both of the riders' mounts were breathing heavily and were grateful for the rest. They seemed even more relieved when the heavy load of rocks was taken from their backs.

Although he was wheezing almost as badly as his tired horse, Doc still managed to heft a pair of the burlap sacks over his shoulders and follow Creek into the cabin. Waiting patiently inside was a slim, older man with a plump face framed by a thin cap of gray hair. The man's beard and mustache seemed like a layer of frosting on a stale cake.

Rising from his seat at the far end of the cabin's only room, the gray-haired man straightened his suit and checked the gold pocket watch hanging by a gold chain from his vest.

"You're late," he said.

Doc allowed the bags to fall to the floor. When they hit they sounded like they'd go straight through the floorboards to the dirt below.

"Creek, Ah'd like you to meet Jeremy Gearson. He's the banker from Chicago Ah told you about, and he's interested in our gold."

"Pleased ta meet ya," Creek said as he set his pair of sacks down much gentler than Doc had. "You don't look like you're from Chicago. From what I hear, that city can be a pretty rough place."

Gearson glanced distastefully at the hand Creek offered before deciding to ignore it.

"I'm originally from San Francisco, but Chicago suits my present needs just fine. It's a growing community with upstanding citizens."

Resting in a rocking chair next to the door, Doc held a monogrammed handkerchief to his mouth and hacked into it. When his breathing leveled out he said, "Ah'm sure you're correct, sir. Fine citizens who meet in secret to buy stolen gold."

The banker shifted uncomfortably but said nothing.

Looking over at Creek, Doc played up the moment.

"Ah just want to be very clear about what we're doing here," he said. "What we have is stolen, isn't it, Creek?"

"That's what the man I bought it from said."

Which was true.

"And it is gold, right?"

"Yep."

Which was false.

"Can we just get on with this, please?" Gearson pleaded. "I know what I'm getting into and I'd prefer to just conduct my business here and leave."

"Of course," Doc said.

"Is that the gold?" Gearson asked, motioning toward the four sacks.

Nudging them with his toe Creek said, "They damn well better be!"

"I'd like to inspect the merchandise, if you don't mind," the banker said.

Doc never objected to stealing or cheating, but he couldn't stand people who refused to live up to their actions. Men like Gearson, who wanted to lie and swindle and tell the world they were "respectable businessmen" never failed to turn Doc's stomach.

This job is going to be more than easy, he thought. It's going to be a pleasure.

Rising from his rocker Doc yanked open one of the bags, removed a nugget, and tossed it onto the table.

"By all means," he said, "inspect away."

Gearson's eyes flicked to the table and back to the bags on the floor. Striding over to the one closest to Creek's feet, he pulled open the drawstring and drew a rock from deep inside the sack. He then placed that one on the table and looked at Doc as if he expected a reward for creativity.

"This one will do," he said.

After leaving Duke by one of the trees far from the trail, Clint scouted ahead on foot. The tracks had been easy to follow, keeping to a dirt path and not veering off until they'd come to within a half a mile of a small lake. From there, they'd headed for a solitary cabin built along the water's banks.

Next to the horses ridden by Doc and Creek there was a third. After making a quiet search of the grounds surrounding the cabin, Clint could find no trace of another person, so he assumed everyone was inside and took a chance on inspecting the horse and saddle.

Judging by the gear on the third horse, its owner was well-off and a stranger to the open range. By comparison, the animals belonging to Doc and Creek were old veterans of the trail. Other than that he found nothing that could help him.

Clint crouched next to Creek's horse and thought about what his next move should be. Before he could make any decision, the sound of another rider approaching from the woods echoed faintly through the clearing. Knowing he had about five seconds to make himself scarce, Clint hurried away from the hitching post to crouch behind a nearby clump of bushes.

THIRTY-EIGHT

Inside the house Gearson produced a leather pouch from a satchel lying underneath the table. It resembled the one Doc kept in Hyman's back room and contained the same kind of materials. Looking confident that he was in control of the situation, the banker opened his gold testing kit and set his tools out on the table.

Only Gearson's swift, practiced movements as he removed a blade and the vial of acid seemed to occupy his attention. For the moment the other two men in the room might as well have ceased to exist.

Doc hovered over Gearson's shoulder, shifting on his feet and digging in the pockets of his black overcoat like an impatient child. Taking the part of experienced parent, Gearson paid the gambler no mind.

"You got anything to eat in this place?" Creek asked as he rummaged around the back of the cabin.

For a second, Gearson looked away from his work.

"No, but there's a pump outside if you'd like something to drink."

Creek Johnson made a face and said, "That's not what I had in mind."

Gearson's hands moved expertly over the nugget as he began to slice off a sliver of ore to sample with the acid. Like a craftsman chiseling rock out of raw material, the banker neatly shaved off a piece and set the rest of the nugget on the table. All the while, Doc watched over him, hanging there like a troublesome shadow.

"That should do it. I'm sure this test will prove unnecessary," Gearson said, as he shot a glance at Doc, "but one can never be too careful."

"Of course," Doc said. "Ah just love watching a professional in his element, Mr. Banker Gearson. Please continue."

Gearson laid the sliver of rock between his thumb and forefinger and raised it to eye level. He hadn't looked at it for more than an instant when a gunshot exploded from just outside the cabin's front door. A second shot quickly followed, causing Gearson to jump in shock and then drop to the floor, covering his head with both hands.

Without missing a beat, Doc's hands flashed from his pockets to snatch away the little piece of fool's gold from the tabletop. In less than a second, Gearson's sample was replaced with a similar chip of rock that had been hidden inside his coat.

About damn time, Doc thought. That wasn't what they had planned, but it would do nicely.

THIRTY-NINE

From where he was hiding, Clint watched as the rider approached the cabin, dismounted, and started walking toward the door on foot. Clint didn't recognize the man, so he decided to wait and see what his intentions were before making his own presence known.

The newcomer paused for a second in front of the cabin, taking suspicious glances over his shoulders. This was precisely what Clint didn't want him to do. Although the bushes providing Clint's cover were enough to keep him from view, they weren't enough to stand up to any kind of decent inspection.

Instantly spotting Clint, the other man wheeled around to face him while his hand instinctively went for the gun at his hip.

"Who the hell are you?" he whispered.

The man couldn't have been more than nineteen years old and had the shaky eagerness marking someone inexperienced in the use of a pistol.

"I'm a lookout," Clint lied.

"You just stay right there and I'll be right back," he said to Clint.

Keeping Clint in view he started making his way toward the door once again.

Something about the young man didn't sit right with Clint and he decided to run a bluff.

"Why don't you let me check with Doc if you're really supposed to be here?"

For a second Clint thought the young man had bought it, but then the other's face darkened and his posture turned belligerent.

"Doc knows damn well I'm comin'," he said. "I think you're the one who don't belong here."

With that he drew his pistol as fast as he possibly could. His draw was so uncontrolled that he yanked on the trigger before he cleared leather and shot a hole in the ground right near his big toe.

Clint had already drawn but held his fire when he realized how inept the boy was. Now he took careful aim—something you could not do in the heat of a real gun battle—and fired one shot. His bullet struck the boy's holster and it went flying, having been completely torn from the gun belt.

The boy still held his gun but dropped it when he realized what had happened.

Clint moved swiftly, snatching the gun from the ground and clubbing the boy over the head with his own weapon. It was not something he liked using his own gun for. Pistols were meant to be fired, not used as clubs. It tended to dent them in vital places.

Stooping to examine the unconscious boy, Clint was satisfied that he would be nothing to worry about for a while.

"So much for the subtle approach," Clint muttered as he walked toward the cabin and waited for the front door to burst open.

• • •

Doc hid the piece of fool's gold he'd snatched from the table deep inside one of his pockets before kneeling down to where Gearson was cowering on the floor.

"Don't fret, now," Doc said. "Creek and I will check this out. It's probably nothin'."

Signaling for Creek to cover him, Doc stood and made his way to a small window next to the front door. He looked outside and immediately saw Clint Adams standing over the unconscious body of Jimmy Conway. Doc shook his head, marveling at how the young man had managed to mess up such a simple task as had been paid out for him.

Creek Johnson stood on the other side of the door, waiting for Doc's signal to move outside. It was given, along with the signal to put up his gun. Still unsure as to what was going on, Creek did as he was told, holstered his weapon, and opened the cabin door. Doc stood next to him and leaned over to whisper into his ear.

"We don't know who Jimmy is. Just act dumb and don't worry. I already made the switch."

Both men put on expressions of casual shock and strode outside.

"What brings you here, Adams?" Creek asked. Both men ignored the unconscious boy.

Motioning to the fallen boy Clint said, "I found that one sneaking up on you and tried to ask him what his business was. He decided to draw on me, instead."

"He's dead, then," Doc said.

"No," Clint said, "I didn't have to kill him to stop him."

"Ah don't believe that answers Creek's question, Clint. What are *you* doing here?"

"I was giving my horse a chance to stretch his legs

and wound up here. When I recognized your animals tied up in front, I stopped for a moment, and that's when junior here came along. The rest happened just like I told you."

Doc walked over to where Conway was lying and looked down at him.

"Any idea who he is?" he asked.

"I was going to ask you the same thing."

"Creek?" Doc asked. "You know him?"

"Never saw him before," Creek said, which Doc recognized as a mistake. From where he was standing Creek could not see Conway's face.

Creek came over and nudged Conway with his boot.

"Probably just some robber thinkin' we was easy marks out in the middle of nowhere." Looking at Doc and Clint, he grinned. "I'd say he was about as wrong as he could be."

"Looks like we owe you a drink, Clint," Doc said. "Care to step inside for a bit or should we meet back in town?"

Creek looked alarmed at Doc's invitation and watched Clint carefully, waiting for his reply.

Clint sensed Creek's tension, and wasn't sure what the man's reaction would be if he accepted.

"What about him?" he asked, motioning to the young man who was still in dreamland.

"Oh, Creek will take care of him," Doc said, turning to Creek. "Make sure he's taken care of."

"Don't kill him," Clint said.

Doc nodded and said to Creek, "Nothing fatal. Just keep him out of our way for a while."

"No problem," Creek said. He stooped and lifted the body up onto one burly shoulder as if the body was weightless.

"Hell," he said, "I doubt he'll wake up before we leave, anyway."

Inside the cabin Jeremy Gearson was already back

on his feet and continuing with his testing. Seeing this as he walked back inside, Doc felt confident that his switch had gone unnoticed, masked by Clint's distraction.

Doc made the introductions.

"Clint Adams, meet Mr. Jeremy Gearson. He's a banker from Chicago and he's buying some gold from us."

Simple truth, Doc decided, was best.

FORTY

The banker didn't look up from his work, merely acknowledging Clint's presence with a nod and a grunt. When the men stepped inside and Doc closed the door, Gearson was in the process of applying acid to his sliver of rock. In a few minutes, Creek entered without his unconscious burden.

Clint knew immediately what was happening here and looked around the room for the sacks he had seen at Hyman's. Sure enough, lying in the corner closest to the front door were the bags. They looked exactly like the ones he'd seen in the back room. Although he admitted they *could* have been different bags, he doubted it.

He watched closely as Gearson completed his inspection, wondering what Doc was up to. Surely a banker would be able to tell—

"Everything seems to be in order here," Gearson said. "Good quality. I'll be wanting to take all of

it back to Chicago as soon as possible. Also . . ."
He looked at Clint uncomfortably.

Shaking his head, Doc dismissed Clint with a wave
of his hand.

"It's all right. You can talk in front of him."

Clint maintained a confused silence.

"Also," Gearson continued, "I'm afraid I'll have to
insist that one of you accompany me to my bank. I'll
pay as soon as I'm safely home with all the gold in
my vault."

"Little insurance policy, huh?" Creek asked.

"If you prefer to call it that, yes. I would hate for
anything to happen to me during my journey." Addressing his words to Doc, the older man's voice
turned hard around the edges, but it was a hardness
tainted by fear. "You fellows do have a reputation."

"You don't have to worry about that," Doc said.
"Ask Clint, here, about reputations. Very damn few
of them are earned. As for one of us accompanying
you back, we can discuss who that will be when we
get back to town—which Ah'd like to do before it
gets colder."

"Very well," Gearson said.

Creek began lifting two of the bags over his shoulders when a few nuggets fell out.

"Allow me," Clint said. He picked up the rocks, set
them back into the bag that was sagging open, and
pulled on the drawstring to close it. No one saw him
palm a smaller one.

Doc followed Creek outside with the remaining
bags and tipped his hat to both men.

"We'll bring our mysterious young friend back to
town, as well. Ah'm sure the law will know this trou-
blemaker on sight."

Clint wanted to ride the intruder back to town himself. He wanted to use the opportunity to question
the young man.

"I'm on better terms with the law in Leadville, Doc.
Why don't you let me do it."

"Suit yourself."

That surprised Clint. He didn't think Doc would go for the idea.

After the bags were loaded onto the horses, Doc and Creek headed toward a clump of tall trees behind the cabin. Following close behind, Clint noticed one of the trees had rope tied around its trunk, down near the base. As the trio got closer it was obvious the ropes were hanging loose and, judging by the amount of slack, there had once been someone tied there.

"Aw, shit," Creek grumbled. "The little rat squirmed his way out. He couldn't have gotten far, though."

Doc kicked the base of the tree and cursed under his breath.

"Ah'd say we could track him, but why bother? Let's get back to town. That may be where he's going, anyway."

"Yeah," Clint agreed, "you're probably right."

Clint's eyes focused on the ropes. With the amount of times they were wrapped around the tree they should have bound the young man so tightly that he shouldn't have been able to move.

Also, seeing as how he would have just roused from being unconscious, the prisoner shouldn't have had the strength to stand up, let alone escape into the woods.

Clint felt sure that Doc and Creek were putting on a performance for his benefit, and while Doc's was pretty good, Creek's was awful—especially claiming not to know the young man without taking a look at his face.

"I'll just look around a little," Clint said, wanting to be alone.

"Are you sure?" Doc asked. "Ah could stay—"

"I'm sure, Doc," Clint said. "You two go back and I'll be along shortly."

FORTY-ONE

Clint didn't bother looking for the escaped kid. That was never his intention. He knew the boy was no professional killer, probably just a backup man for Doc's scheme. He had plenty of time to ride back and decided to take the opportunity to let Duke stretch his legs. As they got closer to Leadville, though, he slowed Duke to a walk and spent a few minutes examining the rock he'd palmed back at the cabin.

It didn't take long for him to realize that it was the same kind of rock he'd found in the back room at Hyman's: fool's gold, also known as pyrite. He wondered how a banker, who had obviously tested one of the nuggets, would not know this.

Clint knew that part of Doc's history was as a con man, but even if he'd managed to fool one man into thinking he was buying four bags of golden nuggets,

163

surely there would be someone along the way who would see the truth, sooner or later.

There had to be more to Doc's plan than what he was seeing. And the only way for him to be certain was to tag along with the banker and his insurance policy back to Chicago. That way, he could see the deal through to the end and find out what Doc had in mind for the pigeon named Jeremy Gearson.

Clint's first stop after returning Duke to the livery was his hotel. He was hoping that the young bellboy who had taken his bag to his room when he checked in would be there. Sure enough, he was leaning against the wall in the lobby with a copy of *The Democrat* in his hands.

He noticed Clint coming and closed the newspaper.

"Afternoon, Mr. Adams," he said eagerly. "Can I do anything for ya?"

"As a matter of fact, you can," Clint said. "What's your name?"

"Andrew, sir. Andy."

"Andy, how'd you like to make a dollar?"

"I'm your man!" Andy said immediately.

"I need you to find out something for me."

"I can find out whatever you need, Mr. Adams," Andy said. He was about fifteen, small and skinny for his age, but eager to please.

"I need you to find out when a man named Jeremy Gearson is leaving town. He should be headed east on the stage, and he might be going with someone else."

"Do you know where he's stayin'?"

"No, I don't. You'll have to find that out, too."

He handed the boy the dollar, which disappeared into his pocket. Then he took out some more money and held it where the boy could see it.

"When you find out what stage he's on, buy me a ticket to the same destination and keep the change. Understand?"

"I sure do," Andy said, happily taking the money.

"When you've done all of that come here and tell me. If I'm not here, wait for me."

"Don't worry, Mr. Adams, you can count on me!"

With that the young man bolted from the lobby and out the front door. Just then Clint realized that all of the riding he'd done had helped him build up an appetite and he headed for Sally's.

"You tell me," Doc said to Creek Johnson. "Is riding up and knocking on a door too hard a job?"

Creek leaned against the bar at Hyman's and started to laugh.

"Seems it's too hard for Jimmy Conway. You gotta admit, though, he was supposed to cause a distraction so you could switch nuggets, and he did."

"Yeah. He also managed to drag Clint Adams into the picture."

"Hey, he went along with everything, didn't he?" Creek asked.

"He'll be bringing it up soon enough."

"What are you gonna tell him?"

"To mind his own damn business!"

"All we have to do," Creek said, "is get that banker on that stage tomorrow at two-thirty. After that it won't be long before Gearson hands over our money."

"If all goes according to plan," Doc said.

"Don't worry, Doc," Creek said. "This is gonna go smooth as silk."

Doc laughed. The very thought of a businessman like Jeremy Gearson paying five thousand dollars for four sacks of fool's gold was more than enough to

brighten his spirits. Only one thing could go wrong
before he left town the next day.

As if on cue, when Doc looked up from his drink,
he noticed that very thing walking through the front
door.

FORTY-TWO

The door to Hyman's saloon nearly rattled off its hinges when Bill Allen came storming through with gun in hand. The lawman stank of whiskey, and his whole body shook with nervous energy as he scanned the room, looking for a target.

"There you are, you skinny son of a bitch!" Allen shouted when he spotted Doc at the far end of the bar. "You've been ducking me long enough, making a fool outta me behind my back. Tonight we settle our score, or I'll shoot you down like the scum you are."

Everyone at the tables between Allen and Doc quickly cleared out of the line of fire, but they stayed in the saloon, wanting to witness what was about to happen. In all their minds, even though Allen had his gun out, they expected Doc to kill the police chief, and nobody wanted to miss that.

Creek Johnson stepped back after a whispered

word from Doc, who finished his drink and turned to face Allen.

"Kind of dramatic for five dollars, don't you think, Bill?" he asked.

"This ain't about five dollars, Doc. It's about respect. It's about you comin' here and thinkin' you can do whatever pleases you, as though you were a . . . a king, or somethin'.'"

"If you think that badge makes you bulletproof . . . you should probably reconsider your actions . . . Chief."

Looking around at the crowd of people watching them, Allen felt as though he were putting on a show for the citizens of Leadville. This was the moment when the law put its foot down on such notorious undesirables as John Holliday. Now was the time for him to get the respect he felt he so rightly deserved.

Allen was holding his gun down by his side. The moment he began to swing it up into firing position, Doc had already drawn his nickel-plated .45 from his shoulder holster. Allen's thumb had just pulled back the hammer of his .45 when Doc fired, sending a bullet across the room and into the police chief's gun arm, just below the wrist.

Allen's right hand jerked backward as if it were yanked by a rope and his gun flew underneath one of the nearby poker tables. For a second, the wounded man just stood there, looking more shocked than anything else. Then he dropped to the ground with his bloody arm clutched to his chest, his teeth bared in a painful grimace.

Inside the saloon the only sound was Allen's groaning as he lay on the floor. Outside, however, hurried footsteps drew closer, sounding like thunder as two pairs of boots pounded along the boardwalk toward Hyman's.

●　　●　　●

Clint instinctively knew what had happened at Hyman's. It had all been coming down to this. When he heard the shot he hurried to the saloon, and saw that he was only a few steps behind one of Chief Allen's young officers. If the man ran into the saloon half-cocked, Doc might kill him, and that would be bad for everyone.

The officer ran into the saloon, followed closely by Clint, who took the scene in quickly. Allen was on the floor bleeding, but he wasn't fatally shot.

"You son of a bitch!" the officer shouted and charged toward Doc with his gun drawn. Doc's gun was still in his hand. His face was cool and collected, but Clint knew he'd kill the young man if he felt threatened.

Clint closed on the deputy quickly, grabbed him from behind, spun him around and disarmed him.

"You're interfering with the law, mister," the young officer shouted.

"I'm keeping you alive, son. Let's just find out what happened here."

"Holliday shot the chief, and I was keepin' him from finishin' him off."

"If Ah wanted to finish him off," Doc said, leaning against the bar, "he'd be dead."

"He's the law!" the officer said.

"He came after me regarding a personal affair," Doc said. "I wasn't even placed under arrest."

Clint looked around at the crowd of people who had watched the whole thing.

"Is that true?"

"It's true," Creek Johnson said. "Allen came in waving his gun. Doc defended himself."

"Anybody else?" the young officer asked.

Reluctantly two men and then a third came forward and backed Creek's story.

"It's common knowledge there's bad blood between these two," Clint said to the officer. "Let Doc stand trial for what he's done. There are plenty of witnesses here."

Reluctantly the police officer nodded and accepted his gun back from Clint. Two more officers entered the saloon at that point, and Doc willingly gave up his gun, not wanting any more trouble.

Two of the officers helped Bill Allen to his feet. The third—the young man who had come in first—looked at Doc.

"You better not try to skip town, Doc."

"Ah'm not going anywhere, sonny," Doc said.

"Doc?" Clint said. "Can we talk in private?"

"No more private talks, Adams," Doc said. "They're wearing thin."

Creek came up and stood next to Doc.

"I kept you from killing that young man, Doc, and maybe I kept you out of jail," Clint said.

"Yeah, maybe."

"You are going to stay in town for the trial, aren't you, Doc? You're not going to Chicago with Gearson?"

"Creek'll do that," Doc said. "Ah'll stand trial. Ah've got enough witnesses that'll say Ah defended myself."

"Good," Clint said, "then I'm out of it."

"Good," Doc said. "Ah never wanted you in it."

Clint left the saloon, still planning to be on that stage tomorrow. Doc would probably get away with shooting the chief of police—he doubted a judge would even try him, given the personal history of the two men—but he wanted to see the man's fool's gold scheme through to the end.

FORTY-THREE

Watching from across the street, Clint waited until the stage was about ready to leave before approaching with his luggage. The bellboy at his hotel had succeeded in getting him a ticket, but he didn't want Creek or Gearson to know it until the last moment.

As he drew closer, leading Duke, he noticed the four burlap sacks strapped to the top of the coach.

"Hold up! I'm coming," Clint called out.

Looking out from the small rectangular window, Creek Johnson's unruly beard rustled in the wind and an uneasy scowl crept onto his face.

"What the hell are you doing here, Adams?" Creek asked.

Clint tied Duke to the rear of the coach and handed his single bag up to the driver.

"I'm headed east to meet up with a friend of mine. Helluva coincidence, isn't it?"

"Yeah," Creek said. "Damn spooky."

Creek obviously didn't like this development one bit.

Good, Clint thought as he climbed aboard, he wasn't supposed to like it.

Built more for long hauls than the stage Clint had taken from Cedar Cross to Denver, this one jostled and bucked with only every second hole in the road. In the back of his mind, Clint swore it would be a long time before he stepped onto another stage after this was all over.

Jeremy Gearson sat rigidly next to Clint, looking as though he were on his way to a bank robbery. There was a middle-aged man sitting next to Creek Johnson, who had fallen asleep soon after they'd left Leadville.

There wasn't much conversation among the four men. The stranger remained asleep, Creek didn't feel like talking, and Gearson certainly didn't want to discuss his business with anyone. Clint was satisfied with the fact that his presence there seemed to be making both men uncomfortable, so he didn't bother trying to get them to talk.

"Hear that?" Creek asked suddenly.

Clint did hear it. It was the sound of riders, and it sounded pretty nearby.

"They're right over there," Creek said, looking out his window. "See 'em?"

It took a moment, but Clint finally did. Two men on horseback were racing toward the stage as fast as their mounts would carry them.

"What is it?" the stranger asked, waking up. "A robbery?"

"Don't know yet," Clint said.

He could see that both men were holding rifles in their hands, and he found it odd that there was something familiar about them.

"They look familiar to you, Creek?" he asked.

"Nah," Creek said, "not to me. They sure are comin' fast, though. We better be ready."

"For what?" Gearson asked nervously.

"For anything," Clint said, drawing his gun.

The riders intercepted the stage and forced it to stop. It was then Clint recognized the men as the same men who had pulled Arlo Gentry from the stage from Cedar Cross to Denver. He also noticed they had a third, riderless horse with them.

They were marshals.

"I'm looking for Jeremy Gearson," Marshal Klellan called out. When he saw Creek's face in the window, he smiled and added, "You, too, Creek. Everyone else stay inside. This ain't your affair."

Creek climbed out first, and then Gearson nervously clambered over Clint to get out. This time Clint was close enough to hear the conversation.

"Where's the gold?" Klellan asked.

"What gold?" Creek asked.

"The gold that was stolen from Fennelly's prospecting team two weeks ago. We caught Charlie and his partner two days ago, Creek, and they told us they sold it to you."

"There's got to be a mistake here," Creek said, holding his hands out in front of him and then dropping them to his sides. The minute his hand came anywhere near his gun, the second man with Klellan raised his rifle and held it ready. Clint couldn't make the man out from where he was.

Creek moved his hand away from his gun carefully.

"Like I said, there's been a mistake," he continued. "This gold is not even real."

Clint frowned. Was Creek that scared that he was giving this fact away in front of Gearson?

"What?" Gearson hissed, shocked.

Klellen started to laugh as he produced a pair of shackles from one of his saddlebags.

"I doubt our good banker here would pay good money for fool's gold. Anyway, real or not, that stuff is stolen property and both of you are under arrest."

"What?" Gearson asked, shocked again.

"You'd best keep quiet, banker," Klellan said. "Creek, toss your gun over and then bring those bags down off the stage. Move!"

Creek did as he was told, tossing his pistol to the dirt in front of Klellan's feet, and then climbing up on the stage. The burlap sacks thudded to the ground heavily, followed by his bag and Gearson's.

Klellan supervised the transfer of the sacks to his horse, as well as the second man's animal. This was when Gearson started to panic. He began to shift from one foot to the other, as though he were trying to decide which way to go, but he was so panicked he was rooted to the spot.

Clint was still trying to get a good look at the second rider with Klellan, but because the man was situated by that time with the rifle blocking his face, he couldn't make him out.

Klellan made sure to take care of Creek first. In under two minutes Johnson was cuffed and placed astride the riderless horse. Gearson, now shaking and muttering to himself, took less time to handle and was soon shackled and placed in the saddle behind Creek.

All the while Gearson could be heard mumbling to himself, "I can't go to jail. I've got a business, a family. I can't go to jail."

"Shut the hell up," Creek growled. "Hold yourself together and I'll handle this."

When Clint heard this he slowly climbed out of the stage and took a step toward Klellan. As he anticipated he was immediately put in the second man's rifle sights. He held his hands out in a peaceful gesture.

"You're Marshal Klellan, right?" he asked.

Klellan squinted at him.

"That's right. What do you have to say?"

"I'm Clint Adams, Marshal. I was just wondering if you needed help with these two."

"Clint Adams . . . the Gunsmith?" Klellan asked.

"I've been called that. You know who I am, so you know I can help you."

"If I needed help, Adams, you'd be my man. Fact is, I don't, but thanks anyway."

With that Klellan mounted his horse. He rode up to Creek's mount, grabbed the reins, and led it away, followed by his partner, who was now showing his back. Clint never did get a good look at him.

Clint watched the riders disappear behind a small range of hills. He knew what Creek had meant when he told Gearson to let him handle this. He was going to bribe Klellan, who Clint already knew was a crooked lawman. Of course, Creek was a handy man with a gun, and a valued partner of Doc Holliday. He might have been planning an escape, in an attempt to keep the gold from Klellan.

Either way, Clint wanted to be there when the move was made.

He retrieved his gear, tied it to his saddle, and mounted Duke, waving at the stage to be off. Then he picked up the tracks of Klellan and company, and began to trail them, figuring to keep a discreet distance so they wouldn't pick him up.

FORTY-FOUR

After half a day's ride the group approached a small, filthy-looking town. Creek figured they were going to stop there to take care of business.

"This is our chance," he said to Gearson. "Did you bring the money?"

"What money?"

"The money to pay for the gold—and keep your voice down."

"I—I've got some of it."

"Some?"

"Most."

"How much is most?"

"I—I've got four thousand."

Creek frowned. It was supposed to be five, but this would do.

"That's enough," he said. "Now listen—"

"The merchandise," Gearson interrupted, "is it really fake?"

"Of course not," Creek lied. "I just said that hoping they'd let us go. Now shut up and listen. We don't have much time. The money you brought should be enough to dangle in front of these lawmen to let us go."

"You mean bribe them?" the banker asked, his eyes wide.

"Well, we sure as hell can't shoot our way out."

"But . . . that means we'll lose the money and the gold."

"Would you rather go to jail?"

Creek felt Gearson start behind him. The banker was afraid of jail.

"All right," the man said, "let's try it."

They rode into the town and the two lawmen dismounted. Klellan approached Creek and Gearson, while the other man took care of the horses.

"Let me do the talking . . ." Creek said to the banker.

It was two-thirty the next afternoon when Clint walked into Hyman's and swatted the trail dust from his clothes. Just as he'd figured, Doc was sitting in his usual spot behind the faro table, which had not started doing business yet.

"I think you misplaced this," he said, handing Doc something.

The white handkerchief was still dirty from where Clint had found it lying on the ground in an alley of a small, filthy town that didn't even have a name. He'd tracked Klellan and his partner there, but they were gone, as were Creek and Gearson. The tracks in the ground told Clint all he needed to know, along with the handkerchief he'd found.

The "JH" stitched into it was the final clue.

Doc looked down at the handkerchief for a moment before reluctantly reaching out and taking it. It still had some of his blood on it.

"Gonna be the death of me yet," Doc muttered, and then started coughing into the dirty rag.

Although Clint had never been able to get a look at Klellan's backup man, he had been able to see his horse. He didn't place the animal until later, when he remembered that he had seen it in front of the cabin where he'd found Doc and Creek with Jeremy Gearson.

"You were Klellan's backup man, weren't you, Doc?"

"Ah was supposed to be the one riding the stage," Doc said, "but after that business with Allen, Ah couldn't very well buy myself a ticket, could Ah?"

Clint was surprised by Doc's honesty.

"Where's Creek?" he asked.

"You just missed him. Ah don't even know where he went."

"And Gearson?"

A wave of coughing tore at Doc's chest and throat. Today, more than any other time Clint had ever seen, Doc's consumption seemed to be getting the better of him.

"Who cares where Gearson went?" Doc asked, when the coughing had finally subsided. "He's out of our hair and grateful not to be in jail."

"So the whole plan was to scare him into thinking that handing the money and the gold over to Klellan would keep him out of jail."

"It seemed the best way to make a profit from a bunch of rocks, even after Klellan took his cut."

"Why are you admitting all this to me?" Clint asked.

"Look at me, Adams," Doc said. "My days of riding hard and running scams are over. After this Ah plan on checking myself into a sanatorium in Glenwood Springs. You might as well hear the rest, because you figured most of it out, anyway."

Shaking his head Clint took in the sight of John

Holliday. The man had spent most of his life being eaten alive by consumption, but had managed to pack more living into his years than most men could in ten lifetimes.

Doc wasn't the man he had been in Tombstone, and Clint somehow knew that the Georgian would never leave Colorado alive.

FORTY-FIVE

It took just over two weeks for Clint to locate Marshal Bill Henderschott in a town about three miles south of Cheyenne, Wyoming. He'd been trying to locate the man in order to give him a few juicy tips on where he could find some crooked lawmen.

As he rode into town, however, Clint was thinking about something he'd read in a newspaper recently. Doc Holliday *had* gone to trial in Leadville. It had become a big story, involving two high-profile men shooting it out in front of dozens of witnesses.

What made even bigger waves was the news that Doc had been acquitted.

Apparently, all of the men in Hyman's—those who came forward—had testified that Allen had come in to provoke Doc and had never placed the Georgian under arrest before drawing his gun. That, added to the fact that Doc's bullet hadn't done more than break a bone in Allen's wrist, was enough to keep Doc out of jail.

After the trial, Doc had stayed true to his word and left Leadville for Glenwood Springs, a quiet Colorado hospital drenched in clean mountain air. Clint wished nothing but the best for Doc Holliday, but feared the worst.

For the moment, Clint's business was to do something about the only lawmen he knew to be crooked. Marshal Klellan and his deputies must have taken enough bribes to become rich, but Clint knew men like that would never slow down until they were forced against a wall.

Tracking down renegade marshals still wasn't Clint's job.

It was Bill Henderschott's.

As he rode up to the whorehouse where Henderschott was known to be staying, Clint smiled to himself, confident that he'd decided on the right man for the task of cleaning up the area's dirty law enforcers.

Henderschott was always looking for a good crusade.

In about two minutes, he was going to have one.

Watch for

SHOWDOWN AT LITTLE MISERY

3rd GIANT novel in the exciting GUNSMITH series

Coming January 1998 from Jove Books!